Dolores & Fred —

Beloved mom & dad

from your old pop

Wm Neill

May 21, 1990

FLESH

Also by Gus Weill

NOVELS

Fuhrer Seed
A Woman's Eyes
Paradiddle
The Bonnet Man

PLAYS

Geese
Parents and Children
To Bury a Cousin
The November People
Rosenfeld's War

BIOGRAPHY

You Are My Sunshine

POETRY

a couple of local boys
Love and Other Guilts

GUS WEILL

FLESH

ST. MARTIN'S PRESS NEW YORK

DESIGN BY JUDITH STAGNITTO

Library of Congress Cataloging-in-Publication Data

Weill, Gus.
  Flesh / Gus Weill.
      p.   cm.
    ISBN 0-312-04316-3
    I. Title.
  PS3573.E388F57 1990
  813'.54—dc20   89-78026

First Edition

10 9 8 7 6 5 4 3 2 1

To LeAnne, beloved

"Why, Grandma,
what big teeth
you have."
"The better to
eat you with,
my dear."

—*Little Red Riding Hood*

ONE

A little bit about me, but not too much, because who I am is not that important. It's what happened to me.

I was born and spent most of my life in one of those quaint New England towns where tourists come to watch the leaves turn. I admit that we natives didn't notice it all that much and we spent a whole lot more time watching the tourists than the leaves—and wondered what happened to all those snapshots they took.

My father was a career employee of the Social Security Service. I never knew exactly what it was he did. He was a quiet, pipe-smoking man whose grunts and uh-huhs my mother and I could interpret so proficiently that for us his conversation seemed fluid if not voluble. Mostly I remember the top of his head, over the newspaper, wreathed in pipe smoke, and his fingers, which were blunt like little clubs.

This quiet man dominated us with silence, though it was my mother who influenced our lives.

She taught piano and was a frustrated opera singer. She loved to sing and you still could tell that once she had had a lovely voice, a mezzo. And she could tap-dance, this only when my father wasn't around. She could play the piano like a pro.

And so I guess—no, I know—it's all her fault really. My dreams.

She taught me music the way the Mets first baseman was taught baseball by his dad. I had no singing voice (good-bye, Caruso) and was only fair at the piano, but I did learn music. I even did a little composing, and visions of prodigy rang in her head. My son's Fourth Concerto, you know.

Alas, it was the words that I really could handle and by the time I was thirteen, we—Mama and I (I am quite certain my father thought us a little mad, though he never grunted so)—decided that I would be a lyricist. No, not a lyricist, *the* lyricist. Broadway, where else?

I can see my father smiling behind his newspaper, though I never actually saw him, you understand.

I threw myself into the dream, had no time for other high school activities, and, once a year, with her money from piano lessons, Mama took me to New York. For a solid week, we saw a couple of operas and every new Broadway musical. We were quite practical even in the application of abstracts, meaning dreams.

After, over deli, we'd talk and talk and chew big pickles and always arrive at the inevitable conclusion that someday, one day, I would do better than what we had just heard. We had no doubts at all.

Did Sondheim have any idea at all that his successor was at that very moment eating pastrami at the Carnegie?

We lucked out. About 150 miles from home was Whitemore. Yes, that one. The most expensive one. One teacher for every nine students, tuition $18,900 a year, and boasting one of the nation's finest campus centers for dance, theater, art, and, of course, music.

Most of its faculty were performing artists or, like the three wise men, renowned, semiretired, and passing on their genius to students whom they deemed "blessed."

They were recently of the Broadway stage and among them had seven Tonys. One was a writer of books from which musicals had sprung, one was a composer, and one was a lyricist. They were paid extravagant salaries and would accept only seven students in their program, so that was the key: to get in.

At the most, they taught three hours a week, a nugget I could not resist passing on within earshot of my father, who, I feel, shuddered.

Entrance requirements were a four-hour interview (popularly called "the crucifixion" by students) and "a reasonable sample of serious work now under way." Then the three wise men, that's what we called them, would mull it over for half a year and send you a letter telling you quite simply: come, or stay home.

I didn't do too well on the interview. All three yawned and made no attempt to hide it. I was both afraid and intimidated and wished that my mother had come along to quietly move among them and whisper in their ears how talented I was.

It was the book that got me accepted. *Laffin' at the Palace,* my book for a Broadway musical.

The story was relatively simple. The heir apparent to the British throne is dull, very dull. His courtiers decide that somebody has to give him a dosage of personality, like how to tell a simple joke and how to make small talk. His pauses and silences were legendary and his adoring followers no longer perceived them as "his Royal Highness is given to deep thought."

But who to instruct the prince? Wellllll . . . it so happens that a Jewish comic, a Brooklyn boy with his gorgeous Jewish American Princess wife, is playing the trendy clubs in London. So Marty, naturally Marty, is retained to go to the palace, by the back door, to help transform the prince into "a helluva guy."

The prince has a sister and the comic falls for her and it's mutual and now the Jewish American Princess is fighting for her marriage.

That's the basic story, a clash of wildly divergent cultures, strata, and types. And the three wise men liked it, which is how I ended up at Whitemore.

I really applied myself and whenever I stopped even for a breather, saw my mother drumming piano into some kid's fingers, and my breather fled and I plunged ahead.

The three wise men gave me a lot of attention, extra attention, and encouragement, and by my junior year I had a solid piece of work and a bunch of lyrics.

But I had no music to go with it.

TWO

It was a Sunday afternoon. I had dutifully been to church, eaten a hamburger and had a milk shake in one of those tiny cafés along the small main street right outside the college gates, guarded on either side by stone phoenixes, the gift of a rich alumnus who had overcome heroin.

I assumed that the Music Building (gift of a rich alumnus who had overcome the guilt of being born rich) would be empty except for a coloratura soprano whom I coveted in a carnal way but to whom I had never spoken. I was in love with her voice and her charms.

I went into one of those rooms that contained a piano, for a thousandth attempt at composing a melody that didn't sound exactly like Gershwin or Puccini, when I stopped everything at the sound coming from a piano down the dark hall.

Describing that sound is almost impossible, but, as the three wise men often said, the ability to describe things that defy description is what creativity is all about.

Start simply. It was melodic, delicate, touching, and, above all else, not familiar! It got to you, inside you, prodded you, made its point, and then lingered in you. It was like a hummingbird darting into a lovely blossom, backing off with something in its beak but leaving something lovely behind. I did more than listen. I gulped it in as if I had waited a lifetime for that particular sound.

It drew me up off the bench, out of the room, and down the hall, smiling all the while with pleasure.

I walked to the door, which was half glass (built that way to protect the sexual integrity from predators who have been known to occupy music buildings), and peered in.

The man at the piano looked like an old Arrow shirt ad, from another time. Even through the glass, he was inordinately pink, like a bad sunburn in its freshest stages. His hair was light brown, slicked down and parted exactly in the center.

Only his lower lip, which jutted out, kept him from being quite handsome. His lips looked rouged.

He wore an off-white suit that, even to my untrained eyes, had obviously been built on him. His shirt was a pale blue and he wore a very small red bow tie. His suit coat was hung neatly on a chair. His fingers were the fingers of a pianist, long and spatulalike.

I opened the door and stepped in quickly before he could tell me to get out; but he said nothing and continued playing that exquisite music.

He finished, though his fingers remained on the keyboard. His nails were groomed to perfection and buffed. He was exotic.

"Excuse me," I said. "Who wrote that?"

"Me."

"May I listen? It's important."

He shook his head no, smiled wanly, and began to play. The music had subtly changed. Now it was intimate, more internal, and I had the uncomfortable feeling that I was peeping into someone's soul. Now the motif was forlorn, not totally sad, but hinting of melancholy. I grabbed my pen and tablet and words sprang from me to my fingertips and onto the page.

I began to sing and made no effort to embellish my simple lyrics with technique, but let the melody and the words do the job.

When I stopped, he stopped, and the silence became a part of what we had created.

"That's so lovely," I said.

"The words, too."

We shook hands. His eyes were a light green circled by a darker green. His grip was cool, contained none of the passion of his music.

"I am," he said formally, "Justin Caeser."

"And I'm Marion Anderson, with an *o*," I said, cursing my mother for dooming me to this eternal explanation.

"Oh, that one. Professor Claxley told us about you. Called you his 'lost chord.' Said you were free-falling, in space, couldn't find what the *x* equaled."

I resented Claxley's discussing me with other students, but it didn't really matter. "I think I just found it," I said.

"Thank you." He said it so simply. No silly politeness or fake humility. He knew he had it. We had both acknowledged a truth.

"Coffee?" I asked, holding my breath. This was very important to me, like a matter of life and death.

He closed the piano with formality, stood, and I helped him into his jacket, like a manservant. He accepted my attention as if it was the most natural thing in the world and we went out into a dying Sunday.

Sundays do die differently. I thought we would walk,

but he said, "Let's drive," and led me to a big red Buick convertible.

I was self-conscious riding in it. It was loud and ostentatious and not like its owner at all.

"Some car," I said, and again he thanked me and I wondered how his formal politeness would wear on me.

But it really didn't matter. I had found my man. Marion Anderson wasn't free-falling anymore!

THREE

I ordered coffee; he asked for a cup of hot water and a wedge of lemon. He smiled that wan smile and took a tea bag from his coat pocket. "I'm very particular about what goes in me," he said. I wondered whether he was gay. It wouldn't matter, but I did wonder. "An eccentricity, I'm full of them," he said.

I told him about me, showed him some of my lyrics. He studied them quietly. His eyes were guileless. Except for that pendulous bottom lip, I now found him quite ordinary in appearance. Mannered, to be sure. Nobody slicks down his hair and parts it in the center like that.

"You make me think of the past," I said, and then asked him about himself.

He had studied composition in Paris and had a degree from Julliard. He was attending Whitemore for the same reason as I: the three wise men.

"Do you think them well named?" I asked, still angry at Claxley and hoping Justin would say something derogatory about them.

"To a point. I've sucked up all their wisdom." He began sipping his tea. Quietly.

That coming from anybody else would have sounded outrageously pretentious. From him, it was said so simply, so factually, I found nothing offensive. "I'm not quite at that point," I said.

"Oh, you can write," he said, and won me. I love compliments, had been weaned on them.

"Tell me about your show," he said.

"*Laffin' at the Palace,*" I said. I enjoyed saying the words; they made me feel as if I had created something tangible.

"*Laffin' at the Palace,*" he parroted. For no reason, we laughed, at which time, somebody played the jukebox and I found myself shouting the story line over Sting. He won.

"Let's go to my place," he said.

I paid for the coffee and he left the exact tip.

He lived in a condo across the highway from the best subdivision in town. I had been there before because that's where the three wise men lived.

It was simply furnished, though dominated by two objects. There was a black baby grand Steinway in the living room and a huge white deep-freeze in the kitchen.

"My two passions," he explained lightly, "my music and my stomach."

We settled down, I in a big beige stuffed chair and he lying back on a sofa. He closed his eyes while I told him about my show; his fingers pressed together in a steeple across his chest. He could have been asleep. He spoke without opening his eyes.

"Are you Jewish?"

"Are you gay?"

He sat up. "No, I'm not."

"I'm not Jewish," I said. "Episcopalian. You?"

"Nothing."

8

"Would it have mattered if I was Jewish?" I asked.

"Would it have mattered if I was gay?"

"No. It wouldn't have," I said.

"Your being Jewish would have mattered to me," he said, closing his eyes and stretching out again.

We returned to the safer ground of my book and at some point he sat up, took a gold pen from his coat pocket, and reached beneath a low-slung coffee table for a most unusual tablet, covered in some kind of leather, the likes of which I had never seen before. It was a palish pink, darkened about the edges like a rose petal beginning to die. It was quite ugly.

"What is that?" I asked, pointing.

"You do have a lot of questions," he said.

"I'm so sorry," I said, letting the slightest bit of irritation creep into my voice.

Seconds ticked by while he stared at me. "Specially treated pigskin."

"It's different," I said.

"Aren't we?" he said, and we laughed, the tension broken, as he began questioning me about the show. My show. Outside of the three wise men and my mother, no one else ever had, and I was in my glory. His questions were right on the mark and highlighted what I knew all too well were the strengths and flaws. He jotted notes as I talked and time passed quickly. Through heavy brocaded drapes, I could see that night had fallen. He switched on a lamp right above the piano and I asked him to play his music.

"Get you a beer first," he said, and I wondered how he'd spotted me as a beer man. He returned with something called Schneider from Argentina. I was a Carling man but the Schneider was okay. I sat back, felt rich, drank my beer, and got drunk on his music.

It was haunting, beguiling, and did funny things with everything it engulfed, even the furniture in that room. It was as if an artist had drawn something, identifiable, then smudged all the lines so that the object disappeared and left you with feelings—the object was still there but had gone off into some other dimension and en route had become something more, taunting you to join it.

Even the lighter stuff had something bothersome to it, gorgeous but bothersome. And when wit slipped in, the taunting quality darted in and out of the notes, almost teasing, giving the punch line yet holding something back. I smiled because there it was, and then I stopped smiling because there it wasn't! Had I smiled at all?

The darker moments were great, ominous storm clouds blotting out the sun's presence. Behind the dark, there was no light; something had done something to the universe!

Suddenly he stopped. The music stopped. His shoulders sagged and he said, "I don't know." Was fear on his face?

I wasn't certain that I had heard him. "Huh?"

His green eyes bore into mine. "No agreements, no manly handshakes, no pledges. Let's drift into it, and not even try to define it."

"Oh," I said. "All right."

FOUR

So that's how we began.

He and I and *Laffin' at the Palace*.

In many ways, we were alike and that surprised me. It was obvious that he came from some other extremely wealthy world, a world that I could not even imagine. I wanted to ask him about it; I was beguiled, curious. I have always been curious. I wish I had asked him then. Things might not have . . .

On the other hand, we had much in common; for instance, we had some of the same faults. We were too prolific, I with my words, he with his music. Over the period of a year, we wrote more than a hundred songs! We suffered no blocks. One of us had an idea, some nice words or a snippet of melody, and bingo—a song!

We meshed perfectly and sometimes I felt as if I had known Justin Caeser all my life, which was ridiculous. I wanted to know him but he always managed to deflect my questions, gently, very gently, so that I came away knowing nothing or very little.

I began to mimic him. "We are a very private people." And I'll say this for him, he laughed as much as I did.

We began our day in the Student Union over coffee and tea. Then we went to his apartment, where we sometimes remained for two days, working right through, drinking Schneider and eating steak.

Steak really doesn't do that meat justice. There ought to be some other, more exotic name for it. His deep-freeze was a magical cornucopia out of which came the finest meat I had ever eaten. Now I'm no food nut, but the texture! The quality! I became, in a word, a hog, and Justin was always ready—not ready, eager—to broil me still another one. Medium, thank you. I was the salad maker, which was a joke because the dressing came from a bottle. I was surprised Justin didn't seem to mind. Only those steaks mattered.

That year I gained fifteen pounds and loudly protested, even as I chewed, just barely chewed so tender was that meat, "You're fattening me up for the kill!"

"Never," he responded quite seriously, pointing my way with his fork. He said it so solemnly that I began to laugh and in a moment he joined in. We began to sword fight with our steak knives, then jumped to our feet, marched about the room and chanted, "For the kill! For the kill!"

Such moments kept us from flipping out, so intense had our work become.

Then there were the days when we were super critical of each other. "Didn't Bernstein write that?" I taunted him over one of his songs. He called me "Mr. Derivative." But we never got really angry, because we fit.

It was that simple. My words, his music: seamless. They could have come out of the same person. Where one of us stopped, the other began. We were, in my mother's words, "a match made in heaven."

Jesus Christ. Heaven!

Of course, there were differences. Great and obvious ones. My suits (I had two) came from J. Press, were a couple of years old, while his clothes came from Savile Row, where tailors worked from his dummy.

Prior to meeting him, my diet had consisted of hamburgers, tacos, and pizza. He lived on spectacular steaks. I lived in a walk-up, a dingy paint-peeling dump of an apartment, built around my secondhand Underwood and mounds of paper. He lived in luxury, his world centered around his Steinway, which I gathered was not his only piano. My folks were middle class, his staggeringly wealthy. He told me so, though not in any obnoxious way, and really, for my benefit. "It's so ridiculous for you to pick up a check, so downright silly. The day I was born, I was worth a hundred million dollars, as were my sisters. So, do me a favor, keep your hand in your pocket or someplace. I'll pay."

"But my self-image, my pride," I protested weakly.

"Come on, let's feed your image. You can create one of your salad masterpieces. Memorable to be sure."

"Rich bastard!"

Three wise men pushed us into what was, I guess, an inevitable conclusion. They forced us to define our relationship, to reach a conclusion about what it was we did so diligently. Were it not for them, I do believe we might have gone on forever, writing, composing.

But they wouldn't have it. "There has to be a finish line," the lyricist among them said. The book writer said it less imaginatively: "It's time to put your work together."

"Without seams. I can still hear the seams," Professor Claxley said.

"No stitch must show," the lyricist said.

"A puzzle that was never separate pieces," the book writer said.

"A complete, believable wedge of life," Claxley said.

My collaborator and I looked at each other, both dumbstruck and afraid. We backed out of the room with mumbled thank-yous and separated quickly. We needed space and time and agreed to meet that evening at Justin's.

"We can do it!" I said. I did so want that to be true.

"Of course," he said so coolly I wanted to shake him. Didn't he think so? Dear God, what had we been doing?

"The moment of truth," I said.

"I'm afraid," he said.

"I am peeing on myself," I said, in a pretty fair imitation of his voice.

We laughed and he put my stupid words to music, ending on a great sour chord. I took a big swig of Schneider, gulping down some courage.

"After all, what do we have to lose?" Justin said.

"Oh, I'll probably hang myself, that's all."

"I, on the other hand, will parboil myself, with shallots," he said. This amused him greatly and he actually bellowed with laughter, that big bottom lip trembling.

"Don't forget the pepper and salt," I sang, and he joined in, "And a speck, just a speck, of paprika!" He quickly put our stupid words to music, then I asked him, "Where?" He closed the piano; the merriment vanished from his face.

"Where?" he asked, as if coming out of a dream.

"Where will we work?"

"That," he said, "is the question."

"Some place quiet, phones that don't ring. A piano. Isolation. Time."

"Caeser Island," he said without inflection.

"What?"

"My home. Where I live. You've just described it."

"Well, good. I guess. You look troubled," I said, suddenly realizing how very little I knew about this man with whom I was throwing in my life. Not that I hadn't tried to know more, but he was as good at saying nothing as I was at casually asking everything. Besides, the guy was so talented, so generous, that I simply couldn't press him to the wall. And I hadn't. So I knew nothing. Caeser Island. I knew that.

Let me be honest. I didn't really care where he lived. I cared only about getting on with my book, which had become my life.

"I'll have to find out if I can bring you," he said.

"Of course," I said, but my tone of voice must have betrayed my true feelings: Wasn't I good enough for the Caesers?

"You don't understand!" he cried, standing up and gripping my arm.

"Hey, leggo!" I said. The hand squeezing me dropped away and we both looked at it foolishly. He fell back onto the couch and shut his eyes. I had the feeling he wanted me to vanish. "Look," he said, opening his eyes, a pleading look on his face, as if he wanted to say more but couldn't.

"No big deal," I said, "we can find someplace else. Hey, how about my house? We could kick my father's government manuals under a table and work right in the kitchen."

He smiled and we said no more about it.

"Hey, I'm hungry," I said.

"Do you know you sound like a Caeser?"

14

I didn't know. Not then.

The next morning, he was not at our usual table in the Union. I called his apartment. No answer. I walked there, opened the door with a key he had given me, saw the place obviously empty, and went back to my apartment, where I tried doing some writing but couldn't. I was both hurt and irritated. I was spoiled, too, had gotten used to his constant companionship and the work that poured from our collective efforts.

I was, I think, like a horse that is accustomed to pulling a buggy alongside another horse. Suddenly, the other horse isn't there and whatever the remaining horse does is wrong, not balanced, out of sync. In other words, nothing came from my typewriter.

By the second evening, he still had not returned and I found myself overwhelmed with the need for one of his steaks, compensation, I rationalized, for his unexplained absence. I went to his place, flipped on the light over the range, and in the freezer searched about for a rib eye. Then I noticed something, something that I had never noticed before.

Each package of meat, professionally wrapped in butcher's paper, was labeled in somebody's handwriting in green ink, a set of initials.

"L.C. Gonna cook me an L.C.," I said aloud with a rural snicker, even as I foraged about the packets. They were all labeled that way.

"L.C.," I muttered when something touched my shoulder, scaring all hell out of me, and I whirled about to find Justin standing there smiling at the rib eye I held between us like a shield.

He took it from me. I asked, "What's an L.C.? Lonesome Cow?"

"No. It's the code for a particular herd in Argentina. Furnish our meat. Have for years."

"Oh," I said. That sounded right to me.

"Now make a salad," he said. "A Caeser salad!"

FIVE

The so-and-so kept me in suspense. He talked about the weather over supper. It was starting to get cold. "I didn't know that," I said.

He nodded. "The *Farmer's Almanac* says it'll be the coldest winter in a hundred years."

"Have you been hit on the head with a Schneider?" I asked, pushing my empty plate away.

He threw back his head and laughed, slapping the table to emphasize his mirth. Wiping his eyes, he said, "Okay, okay, I'll stop."

"Stop, hell! Start! Tell me where you've been."

"Guess," he said.

"Mars. There's definitely something Martian about you."

"Farther. Much farther. Guess again," he said.

"Pluto. And I'm out of guesses."

"Caeser Island," he said.

"What a fool I am. I never even considered it."

"And," he said, leaning across the table as if he was sharing a secret, "we're set!"

"It's okay," I said, my voice breaking as it used to when I was a boy.

"It's just fine," he replied.

"Wow."

He sat back. "Is that all? Just wow?"

"Well, naturally, I'm curious, too."

"Oh, please don't be that way," he said.

I could see that he was quite serious. "What way?"

"Curious."

I brushed that aside with a sweeping gesture of my fingers. "I mean, well, it was so iffy; you didn't know if it was okay. I guess you meant if I'd be accepted," I said.

He grinned. "No! That wasn't it at all. Oh hell, what's the difference anyway. It's set. We go!"

"Hold on, Justin. I'm not a chess piece. You just can't move me about the board at will. I need to know what it is that would make our working together at Caeser Island such a big deal. I'm sorry but that's the way I am. I believe my father's that way with people who violate his precious regulations."

"Curious."

"Just about important things. Like me," I said.

I followed him into the living room and took my accustomed place in the big chair while he sprawled out on the couch.

"I don't know where to begin," he said, and it occurred to me that we resembled psychiatrist and patient. Very unprofessionally, I took a big swig of Schneider and said, "Just begin."

He looked back at me. "No great mystery. You're going to be very disappointed when I explain, which in itself makes me uncomfortable. Explaining, I mean."

I bet it did; the Caesers didn't like being pressed on anything. I said nothing. He sighed.

"First, it has nothing to do with you. It could have been anybody. It's us. My family. I don't know how to say it. I've never had to."

"Try to just say it," I said in all my wisdom. I liked being a psychiatrist. Other people's mysteries are intoxicating.

"Very well. We're different."

"That's how most of us would like to think of ourselves," I said.

He snorted derisively. "Very, very different. We are surely the most private people in the world."

"That's no sin," I said, sounding like a likable priest.

"Certainly not, if you can afford it. Isolation is very costly. We live on that island. It's *our* island. There's a tiny village on the mainland, a bridge over the ocean. And us. It's always been that way. I'm absolutely certain that it always will be that way."

"Eccentric," I said.

"If you like. I mean, we don't feel eccentric. We've lived that way for generations. You see, don't you?"

"Not really."

"It's er . . . it's done things to us."

"Oh. What kind of things?" I asked.

He groaned. "God, I wish you weren't that way."

"What way?"

"Curious."

"I am."

"Curiosity killed the cat," he said, no laughter in his voice.

"Meow," I said. He did not smile.

"Which brings us to the rules of the game." He sat up and faced me.

"Baseball. I feel like I'm getting into some weird baseball game. No ball and three and a half innings," I said.

"Make a good song," he said.

"What kind of rules?"

"If you insist," he said. "And of course you do."

I meowed again.

"Sometimes you are a son—"

"Well, the hell with you, too," I said.

"You don't understand! It's for your own good. If you can't comply, you shouldn't come home with me."

"You mean I *can't* come home with you," I said.

"No. The choice is yours."

"What exactly are these rules?"

"Simple, really. There are places you can go. There are places you can't go," he said.

"Will the giant get me?" I asked.

"I beg your pardon?"

"Sounds like a fairy tale," I said.

"I don't think so. Sounds to me like life. Everything we do has some rules attached; maybe in fine print but definitely there. We don't follow them and . . ." His voice drifted off.

"You frighten me, you know?" I said. I was afraid.

"You are so damned dramatic," he said with a warm smile, as if I were a beloved child.

"Yeah. You're right."

"Then it's okay?" he asked.

"It's okay," I said, standing. "Believe I'll walk home. I need the exercise."

"As you like. Let's leave Tuesday after class."

"Sure. Tuesday."

The temperature had dropped into the thirties as I trudged along, hands buried in my jacket pockets. It was a two-mile walk and I enjoyed the brisk, good-smelling air. I took pains to think about the weather but I wasn't really fooling myself. That's another fault: I can't fool me.

I was thinking about his family and their rules. I guessed that wealth did strange things to people. Like the richest man in my hometown. He was different; both of his kids had killed themselves. Something had happened. They had everything, but something had happened.

I guessed that was the ultimate luxury, having the wherewithal to be different. Now I was taking their position. It was easy. Who was I to judge them? We came from different planets. Besides, I wasn't going to their world to live. I was going to work on the most important thing in my life! I liked the sound of that. Grabbed on to it. Held on to it.

So they had rules? So what? Go along to get along!

Alas, the cliché stopped me. Cold. I was me. I was a thinking creature. Hello, creature. I laughed aloud. Nancy Drew was on the case.

I was in a deep, dreamless sleep when the telephone rang.

"Are you okay?" Justin's voice asked.

"Until you woke me," I said.

"Look, I'm sorry. You were angry. I made you angry and it wasn't necessary. Those rules, you resented them and I can't say that I blame you." He chuckled. "I don't like rules, either."

"Uh-huh," I said. I wanted to get back to sleep.

"We're just crazy. That's all. Crazy," he said. He didn't sound crazy. "You'll be fine. Hell, they'll love you!"

"You're a good man, Justin Caeser," I said.

"You, too, Charlie Brown," he said, and I laughed. I felt I owed him that. He was doing a lot of giving and I don't believe it was his accustomed role. "Oh, before I forget," he said, "what are your measurements?"

"Say what? My what?"

"Clothes, shoes. Your sizes?"

I sat straight up, thinking, Here I go. "May I ask why you want to know?"

He sounded as if he wanted to be exasperated, but he got it under control. "I've got to get you some things; we dress for dinner, winter clothes . . . clothes!"

"As in *appropriate*?" I asked.

"Very well. Appropriate."

"Is that one of those . . ." I began.

"Yes. One of those. A rule. Now gimme!"

I did. He hung up and I lay there in the darkness listening to the traffic swish by. I never did get back to sleep that night. I got up and made coffee, then went to my typewriter and started working.

By 4 A.M., I had some pretty good lyrics. I mean they weren't usable, but that helped me put things in perspective.

And I had a title: "Fools and Rules."

S I X

Tuesday and all good-byes came quickly. The three wise men nodded majestic assent. They would read whatever we sent.

My folks approved. My father mumbled good luck around the stem of his pipe and my mother issued warnings about my manners and eating habits. She talked loudly as she always does when she is sad. I am an only child.

The moon pointed the way up the coast to Maine. Sometimes it was dark and glowered, and sometimes it brightened up like a candle burning inside a jack-o'-lantern. We always could hear the ocean. It was an assertive presence that never backed away.

He drove while I dozed to the blessed music from a public-radio station. Grieg floated in my mind. I heard Justin yawn and I offered to drive. He pulled over to an emergency area and we changed places. I asked him something innocuous, but he was fast asleep. Once he groaned, awakened, smiled in the darkness, and went back to sleep.

I was hungry and pulled into a McDonald's. He lifted his head, stared at the Golden Arches, and said, "Oh, my God."

"Go back to sleep," I said. I knew he wouldn't want any food unless it came from his freezer. We had never eaten in a restaurant. I chalked it up to one of his peculiarities and I've got to admit, I didn't mind his steaks one bit. In fact, they were addictive. I once had told him so and he had smiled mysteriously, or even winked, as if we shared a secret, and had agreed: "Aren't they?"

When we were on our way again and I was well into my burger, he sat up as if I had stuck him with a pin, frantically pushed the window button down, and stuck his head out, as if he was fighting for breath. "That smell is killing me!" he roared in the wind. I quickly threw the rest of the burger out while he sat back and got himself under control.

"I'm sorry," he said, "that smell made me ill."

"You know who you are?" I asked. "You are Mr. Esoterica."

"I said I was sorry. What do you want?" he asked.

We rode for a while in silence, which I finally broke. "Tell me about your family."

"You'll meet them in a couple of hours."

"Aw, come on, Mr. Esoterica, be a good guy like the rest of us."

"I don't know why that doesn't attract me," he said, and we had a good laugh. "Well, what is it you want to know?"

"Just routine stuff, like how many?" I said.

"One daddy, one mamma. Satisfied? Of course you're not. Not near mysterious enough for that insane imagination, is it? What would you like? That I be the last of the Mohicans?" he said.

"Ugh," I replied. He laughed. "You are a pain in the derriere."

"Brothers? Sisters? Uncles and aunts?"

"Oh, very well. There is a mamma bear, a papa bear, two sister bears, and . . ."

"Overbearing you!" I said.

"Family of five," he answered.

"Now that wasn't so painful, was it?"

"Gut-wrenching," he said.

"Better stop or I'll get another burger."

"Don't even say that!"

"Come on, Justin, don't stop. Connect the dots for me."

"My father looks like Santa Claus. Remember the old *Night Before Christmas* illustration? Well, that's my father.

And just as jolly and with a great bass voice. A Chaliapin voice."

"Son of Santa Claus."

"That's me," he said.

"And your mother?"

"They're an odd couple. She's tiny but lovely. Dark, with a hawk's nose and flat, black, burning eyes. She could be a gypsy. A fortune-teller at a charity bazaar."

"You said you had a couple of sisters."

He stared straight ahead but I could tell he was peering at me out of the corner of those green eyes. "The twins. As long as I remember that's how we referred to them—the twins."

"And are they?"

"Oh, yes. Identical. In a way." He closed his eyes. His face was a mask. He must have felt me studying him. His eyes opened and he stared at me, made me feel uncomfortable. There in the shadows, the only light coming from the radio, I sensed, for the first time, cruelty. It was nothing he said and certainly nothing he did. There was hostility, anger, and something else—power. I told myself it was my imagination, smiled at him in unspoken apology for having these thoughts.

"Know what Clarence Darrow said when he was defending Loeb and Leopold?" he asked softly.

"Can't say that I do."

"Even the rich are entitled to a defense," he said.

"Defense? I wasn't aware any kind of prosecution was under way."

He sat up straight; his hands were laced as if he was in prayer or trying to get them under control. "Questions. All these bloody questions."

"Are they bloody? Funny, I could have sworn they were small talk, as in people making conversation, passing the time," I said.

His hands unlaced; he flexed them and lay them in his lap. The mood had passed. He was just Justin again and I must admit, I felt relieved. Something unspoken bothered me.

Now the music was Puccini. Mimi, I believe it was Tebaldi, was explaining that she was just a poor seamstress. Tears welled up in my eyes. I cry every time. I guess because I know the ending. Mimi dies with Rodolfo shouting her name in the garret.

"You are a very emotional fellow," he said, but not in any judgmental way. A simple, flat statement of fact.

"Guilty as charged. But remember what Darrow said."

"Oh, what was that?"

"Even the emotional are entitled to a quick hanging."

"You character," he said, and then I sensed him going tense again. Ahead of us were the wan lights of a village. "Grace. We're almost home."

"Grace," I said.

SEVEN

It looked almost apologetic as we approached, as if it knew that it couldn't justify its being there. A few buildings fronting the street, an occasional light, a handful of people coming and going quietly.

As though answering my question, Justin said, "It exists to serve the island. We are its major industry. The people who dwell here receive the finest medical treatment available in this state and per capita income is higher by far than in any other community. I tell you all of that so that you don't have to ask me. I think I'll deal with you that way, anticipate your questions, answer them, then wait for the next bunch."

"You missed one. Would I like a beer? Yes, I would. Fortification against meeting new people, new surroundings," I said.

"We'll be there in a few moments," he said.

"Look, it's me, not you, who's uptight. I want a damn drink," I said.

We pulled over to a low-slung, barnlike red building. "The local tavern," he informed me. We got out of the car. His face was stony, as if we were on our way into a dentist's office.

Its name hung on a battered sign, the lettering burned into the weather-beaten wood. A small light beamed down on it ineffectually.

YE LAST CHANCE—1760

Below it hung another sign, this one hand-lettered.

RULES OF THE TAVERN
FOURPENCE A NIGHT FOR BED
SIXPENCE WITH SUPPER
NO MORE THAN FIVE TO SLEEP IN ONE BED
NO BOOTS TO BE WORN IN BED
ORGAN-GRINDERS TO SLEEP IN THE WASHHOUSE
NO RAZOR GRINDERS OR TINKERS TAKEN IN

"Is it really that old?" I asked.

"Don't be silly. A ploy for tourists. It was built after World War II by an Italian family. The son runs it."

The smell of old beer hit us as we entered the shadowy premises. A fading picture of Franklin D. Roosevelt hung above the long bar, which appeared to be made of lumber that had washed ashore. There was an American flag, too, with the wrong number of stars and stripes. And somebody named John C. Atooza's honorable discharge.

A few people leaned on the bar. A small table was occupied by a single person—a big, raw-looking woman in a disreputable white smock. I thought, If she's the village doctor, everybody ought to get a tetanus shot.

The bartender, a trim, short, swarthy man, greeted us without inflection, as if he were an undertaker and unsure whether we were a part of the deceased's family. "Mr. Caeser."

"Our genial host," Justin said, not bothering to acknowledge his greeting. "Johnny Atooza." I ordered a beer. Justin didn't want anything.

"This is not a quaint place," I said.

"You insisted on stopping," Justin said. He leaned with his back against the bar, his arms crossed over his chest, staring out, face expressionless.

"Who's the lady in white?" I asked no one in particular.

Johnny Atooza looked at Justin as though awaiting permission to reply. Receiving none, he ventured forth. "That's our Miss Polly."

"Does she always drink whiskey from a bottle?" I asked. I had only seen that on the Bowery.

"Just since she went into mourning," Johnny Atooza said. He was having a highball. "The boy was everything to her."

Someone at the bar cackled, "Was all she had." Why did that sound like a taunt? Who was being taunted?

"What happened to her son?" I asked.

Justin asked softly, "What's it to you?"

"Not to her son, her kid brother," Johnny Atooza said.

And another voice, leaving the tavern, answered, "He disappeared."

Johnny Atooza, sounding fortified from the drink in his hand, said, "Poof! Just like that."

A man with his hand in a dirty white bandage said, "Maybe Captain Kidd got him."

He certainly got me. "Captain Kidd?"

Johnny Atooza, into another highball, said, "It's our other big industry, better than the island, God bless the island," and he toasted Justin. "Better than fishing, better than lumbering, looking for the Captain's treasure."

Justin said, "The local legend. Kidd buried his treasure near here. Gold doubloons, no less. Something to talk about, something to search for when you're a child." He shook his head slowly at the stupidity of it. It sounded harmless to me.

"On an island, an island like yours," Johnny Atooza said softly.

The man in the bandage said, "Course, no one's allowed to look there."

"Enough," Justin said. He said it so quietly that I was certain that only I had heard him, but that was not the case, because all conversation stopped, as if a switch had been thrown, the current cut off. Miss Polly drunkenly echoed him. "Enough." She drank to that, whiskey spilling down her masculine chin, below which was a dirty-looking gray scarf.

"Are you ready?" Justin asked. It was more an order than a question.

"Sure," I said, paying for the beer.

We walked to the door and someone called, "Come back, come back soon," and the room erupted in ugly laughter.

Justin said, "Misfits, alcoholics."

"Wait." I stopped Justin. "I've got to pee."

"I'll wait in the car," he said. "Hurry."

Now Ye Last Chance was quiet and no one looked my way. Over a door was another sign: YE OLD PISSERY. The tiny room was remarkably clean. I stood at the urinal, making the ice disappear, when I heard the door behind me open. I turned my head. It was Johnny Atooza, and his dark skin was an unhealthy red. His lips moved, forming words but making no sound. He appeared to be in an advanced stage of agitation. He thrust his face into mine. I could smell his highball and I could see the hair in his nostrils.

His eyes darted about wildly, as if he was looking for someone, which was ridiculous in that miniscule area. "Listen," he hissed.

"What in the hell—" I began as he grabbed the front of my jacket and jerked me even closer.

"Goddammit, listen! For your life." He let me go, smoothed down my lapels, seemed calmer. "Don't go to that accursed island." He said it quietly, as if he were carrying out an order.

"Are you crazy?" I asked.

Over his shoulder, the door opened and there stood Justin, looking first at one of us and then the other. Justin smiled at me and asked in the most casual tone, "What did that one say to you?"

The bartender's face was a study in terror, eyes bulging from their sockets, Adam's apple bobbing frantically, sweat beading his forehead, which now wasn't swarthy or ruddy at all, but an unhealthy white, as if all the blood had drained down.

"He wasn't saying anything," I said. I don't know why I lied, why I felt any semblance of loyalty to this Johnny Atooza, whom I had never seen before. But I did. I felt closer to him than to Justin. It was an act of disloyalty that at the time I could not have explained.

Johnny expelled pent-up breath through his nose and spittle flew when he spoke. "I wasn't saying nothin', Mr. Justin, your friend's telling the truth! So help me God. Nothin'."

Justin smiled at him. "We'd better go."

Johnny Atooza wasn't finished. He made a futile gesture, as if he wanted to touch Justin. "Really, Mr. Justin, I told him nothin'. No harm meant. Not from old Johnny Atooza, huh, Mr. Justin?"

It both disgusted me and made me sad to see this man many years Justin's senior groveling that way. "Come on, Justin," I said.

Johnny Atooza watched us advance toward the front door, a forlorn look on his face, as if something had been lost.

When we stood at the door, Justin turned back to him. "Be seeing you, Johnny Atooza," Justin said.

We sat silently in the car, as if we had just run a mile. Embarrassment hung in the air. I could almost tell that he knew that I had chosen a stranger's side. I couldn't look him in the eyes.

"I'm afraid I've made a mistake," he said. I remained silent. I felt that the error was mine. "Bringing you here. Please do try to understand, I've never done it before. We do not have friends; we have people who need us and who can perform services for us. Before you, I backed off when I felt the simplest relationship starting. I always felt it was for the best. For all parties. I want to back off now."

"Whatever you say," I said. I felt like a fool.

He picked up on it. "And you've not been much help. Obviously, that stupid wretch—he's a bookie, you know, and, I suspect, the village supplier, as in crack—you chose to back up his silly lie. Don't deny it. And then your incessant interrogations. You want to know everything! And that can't be. A family as old as mine, we've accumulated . . . well, things that don't concern others. Have to do just with us. But you ask and ask and—"

"What's all the damn mystery?" I exploded. "Just what in hell are you talking about? I know you're filthy rich. This is America. There are a lot of rich people, some even richer than you, I bet."

"Not too many. I better take you back," he said, starting the engine.

"Do that," I said.

"It wouldn't have worked," he said sadly, the bluster gone from his voice.

"I agree."

He turned the car around and we headed back in the direction from which we had come. "I'm sorry about the show," he said. "Maybe someone else?"

"Don't worry about it." I had heard all I wanted to hear. Then silence and pinpoints of light from the dashboard illuminating our little capsule.

"What will you do?" he asked.

I chose not to answer him. It was no longer any of his business.

He persisted. "The question is, what will *I* do?"

"Count your money. Live in—what's it called—splendid isolation," I said. The truth is, I was thinking the same thing. What was I going to do?

Suddenly, with a jerk of the arm and gravel flying, he pulled the car over to the side of the highway. "I never had a friend before you," he said. I felt a tug of response but I did the unusual; I kept quiet. More silence. Cars sped by.

"I am rather lonely," he said. I turned and stared at him. I don't believe that in his entire life he'd ever said those words. In his world, such admissions were unnecessary. "Let's do it," he said, extending a hand.

I took his hand. "Yeah, let's do it."

He turned the car around and we were headed back to Grace. We drove through it and suddenly we were at the head of a long wooden bridge. Lights at either end burned dimly. They looked like Chinese lanterns strung for a party and they barely punctuated the darkness.

I wanted to ask him so much. Why the antagonism for him back at Ye Last Chance, now vanishing behind us as we rumbled over the bridge? And that warning? Johnny Atooza had seemed like a madman, a very frightened one, when Justin said, "Be seeing you."

What was I getting myself into? I laughed silently at my question, it was so melodramatic. Something different, outside my experience, was giving off little warning signals, which I chose to ignore. Maybe it was time for new experiences! To what had I ever had to respond except a bad case of flu, a bully who took pleasure in socking me, first and second sex, a few tough academic examinations? That was it. It was so ordered, so structured that it seemed to belong more on a chart than as way stations in a person's life.

Quite simply, I was tripping along a set, almost preordained path of my particular life. But this—and I could not have defined *this*—this was something else. I stole a look at Justin and suddenly he looked at me and our eyes locked.

"It's okay," he said, as if he were reading my mind.

I looked away and asked, "Are we in some kind of tunnel? It's so dark."

"We're riding beneath a canopy of pine and hemlock, trees that have been here forever. Listen, hear that? The ocean. Some sound, huh?"

"It's eerie," I said. He punched me in the ribs with a finger and said, "Boo!" Then I saw the most breathtaking sight I had ever seen.

There was a mountain, or half a mountain, and on it, blazing down at us, what looked like a zillion stars.

"Jesus Christ," I said.

He stopped the car. "My home. It was a mountain and the Caesers removed about a third of the top. They built that home. There are two ways up, this road we're on, and a path in the rear that leads down to the formal garden and to the beach."

The house seemed more a mirage than anything real. Even in the distance, I could see its pink marble elegance set like a diamond in dramatic lighting.

"Justin," I said. I was speechless. Beauty does that to me.

"It's just a house," he said, starting up the engine.

"Like Verdi was a tunesmith," I said.

And we started up to the stars.

EIGHT

Five servants, including the first butler I had ever seen out-side a Charlie Chan movie, stood awaiting us before a massive, carved front door. Our suitcases were taken in and the car vanished. It was as if we had materialized, not actually arrived.

The butler was a mean-looking shrimp of a man who didn't have an English accent. He bowed and said with no inflection, "Welcome home, Mr. Justin."

Justin introduced us and I saw that the butler wore a wig that looked like one. His mouth was set in place, as if he might be an accomplished ventriloquist, with no move-ment of the lips necessary in the formation of speech. "Kingsley has been with us forever," Justin said as we en-tered a great hall decorated in pink marble and carved woodwork.

An El Greco hung casually like my mother's annual and much-anticipated Hopkins Insurance Company calendar. I spotted a Hans Holbein, and in the days ahead I saw a Goya, a Whistler, and at least two dozen pieces of sculp-ture by Giovanni Bologna. Much of their collection, Justin explained, was on loan to the Louvre. "My father thinks it'll help him to buy the *Mona Lisa*," he said. I smiled but I don't think he was joking.

Two mahogany lions, mouths open as if they'd eat you on the way up, stood guard on either side of a staircase that seemed to have no destination. It just went up. To our right were French doors that led to the drawing room, where four people sat or stood, as if posing for a commercial photographer, about a roaring fireplace. This room was three stories high and overhead was a glass skylight at least a hundred feet long. Over the fireplace was a massive mantel that reached to the ceiling; across from where we stood, the wall was solid glass, providing an unobstructed view straight down of the Atlantic, whose sound meshed in a glorious counterpoint with the popping of the burning logs.

Justin's simple sketch of his father and mother was right on target. Mr. Caeser, one hand in his tux pocket, the other casually holding a glass of champagne, strode across the room. By his walk, you could tell the room, if not the earth, was his.

He was Santa Claus in formal wear, a giant of a man, at least six foot five, with massive shoulders and belly. I had the feeling that his huge paunch was solid muscle. He looked fat but not soft. Mr. Caeser was an awesome man.

He hugged Justin, who looked lost in his father's encircling arms. To me, he extended a huge paw. "Welcome, sir, welcome!" He sounded as if he were reciting lines in a Christmas play. His small blue eyes twinkled and his white beard streaked with gray bristled in enthusiasm. His eyebrows grew wildly, every which way. His cheeks were very ruddy, and I would not have been surprised if he had suddenly called out, Now Donner, now Blitzen!

Mrs. Caeser was a striking contrast to her husband, a compact and, I could not help but notice, curvy woman, blessed with an olive complexion and black hooded eyes that made her seem mysterious and even sinister. Her hair was black but streaked with white. On her hand, a diamond the size of a walnut perched almost precariously, so heavy did it seem. About her neck was a black ebony cross encrusted with diamonds along the edges.

She was no less hospitable than her husband and kissed both Justin and me, then stepped back, appraising me from the shoes up, and said, "This one needs some fattening up." For some reason, everyone found this amusing and laughed more than politely, and Mr. Caeser clapped in agreement, bouncing on his small feet like an oversized prizefighter.

"Yes, oh yes, fatten him up," said a man sitting beside the most beautiful woman I had ever seen. He was in his late thirties and looked like the Pillsbury Doughboy. He was a bit on the short side and looked like one of those people who you immediately thought was jolly. I immediately thought he was drunk: little glassy pig eyes beneath damp blond hair, trying to focus on either me or the martini glass he clutched in fat fingers. There was something obscene about the dimples that punctuated his pink open face and I would not have been at all surprised if he had oinked.

If he was a pig, he was an accomplished one. On his hand was a Harvard ring and across his front a Phi Beta Kappa key.

The girl, that girl, was something else. I have no idea what she wore that first evening except that it was red and hugged her body—all but three-quarters of her breasts, which peered out at a world in which they would, for a time, be the center of all male attention.

She was dark like Mrs. Caeser and her eyes were the same green as Justin's. She was overripe, another ounce anyplace else and she would have been obscene, but she didn't have that ounce and was perfect. Black curls framed her heart-shaped face and her lips appeared ripe and wet. She was almost too much. It made me uncomfortable to be in her presence.

Mr. Caeser did the honors as if he were introducing a circus act, the big voice more than filling the gigantic expanse of that room and easily drowning out both ocean and fire. "My daughter Eleanor and her fiancé, Timothy Hedgely III, barrister."

Eleanor nodded imperiously and Timothy hiccuped.

"Kingsley, show our guest to his appointments so that he and Justin can dress for dinner," Mr. Caeser ordered the butler, who had not stopped filling everyone's glasses with champagne. I bowed politely and I thought how pleased Mother would be. The last time I had felt that way was in a class play in whose second act I was beheaded.

I followed Kingsley out of the room, back into the great hall, and to the base of those unending stairs, where I paused for a moment to give the carved lions a friendly pat. They seemed more real to me than the Caesers. "Just how big is this house?" I asked Kingsley.

"Fifty-two rooms, sir, including a surgery, barbershop, and . . ." He didn't finish but opened the door to "my appointments," which were ice blue with guilded moldings and cornices. There was a sofa on either side of a fireplace and the bathroom was gray marble.

Like a bemused tour guide, Kingsley said, "The furniture is Louis XV and it is of inlaid sandalwood. You will note, sir, the bed can be closed off by silk curtains." He opened a closet containing enough new clothes for a family of three, with shoes and assorted boots on the floor.

"Those for me?" I asked. I was like a child in a candy store waiting for the proprietor to leave so I could dive in and indulge myself.

He nodded. "Will there be anything else, sir?"

I said no and thanked him, but when he was at the door, I called him back.

"Sir?"

"Isn't there another daughter?" I asked.

A look of distress showed on his face, then quickly passed. "I'm afraid, sir, any question about the family will have to be posed to the family." He stood there as if he was waiting for my reaction.

I smiled. "Of course," I said.

When he had departed, I stripped and lay in the gray

tub that was about half the size of a handball court. This is the life, I thought, and wished that my mother could see my surroundings. I had no doubt that my father would have found the Caesers quite mad. I didn't think so. Quite rich, that's all, rich, I said to myself.

I was happy! What an opportunity. I would for a brief time experience not life but *the* life. At the pinnacle. I felt like someone on CNN. Marion Anderson at the pinnacle! I was certain this would be the only time in my life that I would get to live a fantasy, conscious that's what it was, but enjoying it, reveling in it, all the same. I sang aloud: "If they could see me now, that dear old. . . ."

I was thinking about New York and *Laughin' at the Palace*. I had no doubt that we would finish a decent draft right here amid all this luxury and then off to the Big Apple and bingo, dream fulfillment time for Mr. Marion! I liked it. I really liked it.

When I had dressed, I studied myself in formal wear, gave my hair one more good brushing, and descended the stairs feeling like somebody!

In the drawing room, the family sat around a table inlaid with semiprecious stones and drank Louis Roederer Cristal champagne, with Kingsley standing by to do the honors.

I could not help but stare at Eleanor. She stopped you cold, made you blink; you weren't certain that you were actually seeing what you were seeing. Mr. Caeser picked up on my reaction—indeed, he studied it—and muttered, "Well now, well." Mrs. Caeser patted his hand either to calm him down or signify that she agreed with whatever he meant. Timothy Hedgely III offered a silent toast and I blushed a hue only a little less red than her gown. She seemed amused, an adorable smile playing at the corners of those swollen red lips.

I was embarrassed, when Justin stepped in and saved me from making a total fool of myself. "Please don't fret. My sister has that effect on everyone."

The family laughed and I joined in, but lightly.

"Now then, gentlemen," Mr. Caeser boomed, "elucidate the strategy for this as-yet-unfinished epic."

Eleanor pouted. "All work and no play . . ."

"All play and no work," Timothy said, "make Marion fat."

"Don't be boorish," Mrs. Caeser said, voice low and sultry, and pinched Timothy's chubby cheek, but with no affection. I believe she was hurting him and when she released his flesh, there were red marks on his pink complexion. He quickly downed the contents of his glass.

"What's to say," Justin said. "We've tons of work."

I stupidly echoed, "Tons."

"I love it. I love it! Creative genius at work in this house. Well, why not? This is a house of creativity. Are we not creative people?" Mr. Caeser asked.

"Oh yes, I would certainly say so," Mrs. Caeser said. Then she suddenly giggled, diamond ebony cross dancing in the light of the fire.

"They are very creative," Timothy said gravely. "They recreate. I mean God creates, but all the Caesers, they . . ." He suddenly stopped as though he had fallen ill from a bout of self-consciousness. Kingsley quickly refilled his glass.

"Well now, we do have the resources, the wherewithal, assured to us by the sacrifice of our ancestors and our own genius. Why not innovation? Eh? I'm sure our young guest would agree," Mr. Caeser said.

Now the family was looking at me, faint smiles on their faces, obviously waiting for my answer. Was anything taken casually here? Did all words demand a reply? I plunged ahead. "Absolutely!" I learned a valuable lesson: The Caesers sought affirmation, approval, agreement. Mr. Caeser was actually beaming at me, rocking back and forth on the tips of his black patent-leather shoes, while Mrs. Caeser, eyebrow arched, stared at her daughter as if to say, What have we here?

"He's adorable!" Eleanor said.

Timothy, who by now I had identified clearly as a lush, nodded and said, "And can only become more so."

Justin said, "Timothy, you drink too much." There was no pleasantry in his voice. It was cold.

Timothy smiled drunkenly. "And eat too much, wouldn't you say? Or is that okay? Perhaps I should increase my food consumption."

Justin turned away, disgust on his face. Mrs. Caeser said, "Our Timothy has put on some weight."

"Timothy is perfect." Eleanor purred and kissed him on the mouth, her pink tongue darting in. I swallowed the bile that rose from my stomach.

"We don't get many guests," Mr. Caeser said, "and that, sir, makes you all the more welcome, the more precious. Justin, how long do you think this project will take? I would hope forever. We need fresh air in this house!"

"Your home is magnificent," I said. I felt the need to respond to his graciousness.

Mrs. Caeser laughed. "Do take your time, Justin, your father needs a fresh audience and your friend appears willing!"

"Here's to forever. Is that long enough?" asked Timothy, raising his glass in a toast that no one acknowledged. I lowered my glass along with my gaze. I felt guilty.

"Our Timothy is writing a great tome of law. Oh, it'll be a great one. Timothy holds degrees from Oxford and Harvard. Honors, a life filled with honors earned. An intellectual, our Timothy. An eternal scholar," Mr. Caeser said.

"I used to be a practicing attorney. Estates. I am an authority on estates," Timothy said.

"Our family is his firm's, shall we say, principal client," Mr. Caeser said.

"Quite right," Timothy said. He seemed to be struggling for some yesterday, some memory of a past that he could not quite articulate.

"He came to us on family business," Justin said. He seemed amused. "Caeser business."

Mrs. Caeser said, "And never left." There was something so final in her voice.

"Well now, sir, could you blame him? Magnificent Eleanor fell in love with him. Love at first sight, eh, Eleanor?" Mr. Caeser asked, leaning forward for the answer.

"No. Not at first sight," Eleanor said. "But certainly I saw the potential. And love came. Didn't it, Timothy?" I was afraid she was going to give him another of those kisses. I was drinking too much.

Timothy sounded cowered, defensive. "I'm just a man like any other man. Eleanor . . . who could resist Eleanor?"

The family looked at me. It was insane; what did they give a damn what I or anybody else thought? How could it remotely have anything to do with them? Kingsley was cascading champagne into my glass. "Nobody!" I laughed with delight and felt exceedingly clever.

"Drink up! Drink up!" Mr. Caeser said, leaning over and squeezing my knee in a great, powerful paw. It hurt.

"For goodness sake, let him go!" Justin said, and his father said, "Alas, I am an affectionate man. I believe I like this boy." He looked at them. "I like him."

"We all like him!" said Mrs. Caeser, and then asked the others, "Don't we? Don't we like him?"

They looked me over as if examining a prize horse and joined in a chorus: "We like him!"

"God help you," muttered Timothy.

Kingsley said, "Dinner is served."

NINE

The dining room was unreal and I saw the Caesers smile as I blinked in astonishment. The room was fifty-eight feet long and rose two stories high, with lighting from four massive chandeliers that hung from single pins.

Mr. Caeser sat at the head of the table—with his wife on his left, looking like some kind of small, compact package of dynamite. I, the guest of honor, sat at his right. Next to me were Eleanor and Timothy; across from us, Justin.

My attention immediately centered on a decanter in Kingsley's hand, from which he poured a taste of wine into Mr. Caeser's glass. It was so elegant and had twin ruby-eyed silver serpents encircling the glowered cut-crystal body and forming a sensual handle. Signed in Cyrillic was Fabergé and below the signature, the Russian imperial warrant and the date 1890.

Mr. Caeser ceremoniously cleared his throat, a sound that began in his stomach and rumbled its way up and out of his mouth, which I was to learn was his way of halting all conversation save his own. It worked every time.

"The wine of the evening, something quite special for our young guest; the white, a 1964 Montrachet, and the red, well the red is really quite something. Château Latour, 1811, the famous comet year."

Everyone clapped politely and I had the feeling that more was expected of the honoree. I said, "Sir, I am honored."

Mr. Caeser nodded approvingly to Justin. "Your friend is a gentleman."

Justin said, "A very talented one. With words."

Eleanor said, "And very handsome in an unfinished way."

Timothy said into his glass of Château Latour, "No doubt the Caesers will finish him." He stifled a giggle into a chubby fist.

His pronouncement was followed by silence and a glare from Mr. Caeser and Timothy got the message. He said, "I mean culturally. This is a cultural finishing school. The faculty, the Caesers." He was both drunk and nervous and spoke too loudly, his Phi Beta Kappa key swinging like the pendulum of a tiny clock.

That decanter never seemed to empty as glass after glass of precious wine was poured as if it were water from a spigot. I decided that the Caesers stayed drunk. There was no way to escape that incessant, exquisite grape.

Then the servants, one for each of us, began bringing in silver platters. There was something so old-time, so opulent about it that you stared at the head of the table as though Nero might suddenly be sitting there, perhaps studying a thumb, prior to turning it down.

What was not brought to that table? Clam chowder, big tuna, baked flounder with tart dressing, tiny boiled potatoes with golden butter, coleslaw and lobsters too big for the platter that held them.

The Caesers seemed disinterested but peered at the swinging door as each platter was brought forth. There was even a tenseness in the air. They were waiting and gave each other little nervous smiles.

Mr. Caeser cleared his throat and Eleanor giggled and Mrs. Caeser patted her husband's hand as though calming him down. Only Timothy was uninvolved and he gazed down at his plate as though in prayer.

Then the door to the kitchen swung open and Kingsley entered as though he carried the lead banner in the Olympic parade. In his white-gloved hands was a magnificent covered silver platter. Like a priest with the Host, he placed it before Mr. Caeser and removed the cover. I looked carefully; it was obviously going to be something very special. The family held its collective breath.

On the platter, a big brown roast simmered in its own rich gravy. The smell was intoxicating and I tried to place it. What rare spices must they use, I thought, so unfamiliar was the scent.

Mr. Caeser, carving utensils in hand, cut into the meat, watched the gravy shimmer down its side, looked at Kingsley, and hissed, "Yessssss." Mrs. Caeser's tongue darted from her mouth and in a most unladylike gesture licked at her own lips. Eleanor squealed with delight. Timothy groaned softly and Justin complimented his father: "Sir, you've done it again!"

That I chose to stick with the stuffed flounder and lobster didn't bother them one bit. Mr. Caeser cut Timothy's meat first. As Kingsley handed Timothy his plate, the family joined in a minor "Hallelujah Chorus": "Timothy first, Timothy first!"

Timothy stared straight ahead, his lips moving but no sound coming forth. I again had the impression that he was at prayer.

Mr. Caeser tapped on his wineglass with a spoon. "Well? Well?" he asked of Timothy. I thought, What in the hell do they want of him?

Timothy half-pushed his plate with that dazzling cut of roast in my direction. "Surely our honored guest should . . ." There was little hope in his voice for whatever it was he was attempting to accomplish.

"We do not dishonor God's sustenance in this house," Mr. Caeser said, then added, "Eat!" I looked about. Was some kind of oft-repeated joke going on? If it was, I didn't get it. Nor did the family find humor, because every face was set in seriousness.

Timothy still seemed unsure, so Eleanor began cutting up his meat and even feeding him bites. These began quite dainty in size, then grew to big, gravy-dripping chunks. Timothy swallowed as if he was in pain. I wondered whether he had a headache.

Then the Caesers plunged into that meat, and *plunge* is not too strong a word. Like ravenous wolves, they devoured that roast. I couldn't get over it. These supremely secure people ate as if it was their last meal. All dinner conversation came to a dead halt. The sounds they made ranged from teeth tearing into flesh, to guttural sounds of satisfaction from deep within the chest cavity, to plain old lip smacking. Nor did anybody seem to care what I, their guest, thought about this peculiar—not peculiar but *uncouth*—behavior. I thought of my mother shaking her head.

Suddenly my attention was captured by the damnedest sight I had seen thus far in my life, a sight that at once repelled and thrilled me.

One of Eleanor's breasts had spilled from her gown and a droplet of gravy lay on her nipple like exotic makeup.

Their reaction definitely made me shy from the roast. There was no reason why—I love meat!—but nothing could have gotten me to eat that roast. In addition, nobody offered me any. In fact, nobody said anything. They ate, and drank wine to wash it down. Now their lips were greasy and Mr. Caeser burped behind a napkin as Mrs. Caeser gave him still another pat on the arm.

I thought I had seen everything, but the bizarre was to reach its height as the Caesers seemed to doze off! How else to say it? They dozed off. Heads fell forward on chests and faint sounds of sleep came from their pursed lips.

I sat there in both shock and perplexity. Timothy smiled at me, not a nice smile. It seemed to say, Well, there you are. I raised my eyebrow in question. Then Mr. Caeser suddenly lifted his great head from his chest and almost as if on signal, Kingsley stepped forward and began refilling glasses from that Fabergé decanter. Now they were all awake. Perhaps two minutes had passed and I wondered whether I hadn't dozed off myself, dreamed it all, awakened, and . . .

No reference was made to their nap and conversation resumed, this time with a compliment from Mr. Caeser to Kingsley. "My congratulations to the chef; that empty platter will tell him more than mere words ever could."

"And there's more where that came from," Eleanor said, putting that adorable breast, gravy spot and all, back inside her bodice.

Kingsley didn't actually say anything but a cautionary sound came from his scrawny throat. Mr. Caeser actually blanched. "Please translate that sound, Kingsley. In English."

"That was it," Kingsley said, as if proclaiming a death. His eyes were downcast and the decanter trembled in his grasp. The family seemed stunned and I suddenly felt ridiculous chewing on my boiled potato. It was no way to note a tragedy, and a tragedy had obviously befallen the Caesers.

"Why was I not informed?" Mr. Caeser asked softly. Then he shouted in a voice that competed with the ocean beating at the shore so far below, "Nobody told me!"

Kingsley was as white as a napkin and behind him his tails did a little jig as he shook nervously. I thought he might die of fright. "It's never happened before," Kingsley whispered hoarsely.

Mr. Caeser nodded slowly and said to no one in particular, "Well now, well now." He was once again quite calm. Mrs. Caeser made the sign of the cross and kissed the ebony symbol that hung from her neck.

"God will provide," she said. "Let us have faith."

Justin was smiling and I did not like my friend's smile. It hovered between triumph and a leer, as if he had just been told a dirty joke. The smile was aimed directly at Timothy, who shuddered. I don't believe I had ever seen an adult shudder before. It was as if a cold wind was shaking him.

Eleanor responded to her fiancé's convulsions and kissed

him square in one of his dimples. I saw her tongue go in, give a peck, a highly sensual one.

Mr. Caeser's bearded face lit up with a smile. "What a lucky fellow you are, Timothy. Loved by a beautiful woman, the most beautiful, part of a noble family and . . ."

Mrs. Caeser, still clutching her cross, said, "Future assured."

"What more could any earthly creature ask of life? Eh?" Mr. Caeser asked.

"The most fortunate of men," Mrs. Caeser said.

"The brother I never had," Justin said, face now straight.

"It's me who's the lucky one," Eleanor said, graciously, I thought.

"To the contrary," Mr. Caeser said. "It's we who are fortunate. We need your Timothy, Eleanor. By God, this family needs Timothy Hedgely the Third!"

The barrister seemed confused, however, drunk to be sure but not that drunk, and his eyes batted furiously, as if he was standing in blinding light.

Mr. Caeser said, "Come, Kingsley, the pudding."

Eleanor stood, hand on Timothy's head. "To hell with pudding. Come, Timothy."

"Now?" Timothy stammered.

Hands on swaying voluptuous hips, Eleanor said, "Right now."

He pushed his chair back from the table, clutched his champagne glass, and followed her from the room. I thought of a pug dog, but then I envied him as I studied her backside shamelessly. It stuck out and moved like heads following a tennis match.

Mr. Caeser slammed a paw down on the table, causing the glassware to jump. "Damn me, the girl's got spirit! When she wants . . . it . . . she wants it."

"Holy Christ," I muttered without realizing I had done so aloud. I was mortified and began a weak explanation-apology. I didn't know the Caesers!

"Marion envies Timothy!" Justin said, his voice going up an octave, and the family smiled my way until Justin began giggling. Then he muffled his laughter by burying his head in his arms on the table. They all laughed. Me, too—kind of.

"Well, why not?" Mr. Caeser asked. "What red-blooded man could look away from Eleanor's, ah, charms?"

"From her abundance!" Justin said.

"What man indeed? Our Timothy is in for an evening that few men could even imagine. Love," Mr. Caeser said.

The family smiled beatifically. Love. Mr. Caeser said, "I'm afraid we've shocked our guest."

"Sometimes, Father, we do go a bit far," Justin said, looking anxiously at me as if asking whether they had gone too far.

"Tell me, sir, have we affronted you?" Mr. Caeser asked. He sounded boyish.

"Me? Of course not!"

"Everything's fine," Mrs. Caeser said.

"We do want you to be at home among us," Mr. Caeser said with a smile that showed his pearly teeth between mustache and beard. "We are, I must admit, a lonely people. Unfortunate but true. Our wealth has isolated us from the world. Alas, has made us suspicious, an unfortunate and even distasteful quality. Suspicious of others. What does this one want? What is that one after? Oh, it can be quite appalling and tends to make one retreat, sometimes dangerously, within oneself or the family circle. That circle is our shield, our armor. The Caesers are close."

Mrs. Caeser had taken her husband's hand. They were obviously a very close couple. "And when one of us meets someone, say by business, like Timothy first coming to the house on legal matters, or in your and Justin's case by mutual talent and purpose, why it's something very special to us! For us. New blood, so to speak, in our very closed and guarded world."

"Does that make sense?" Justin asked me.

I honestly did not know what to reply. My senses were reeling from the splendor, the champagne, and the bizarre behavior that I had witnessed that evening—particularly the endless flow from that bottomless decanter. I looked at my fingers and realized that they were drumming on the table. I stopped.

"Damn me, I like this young man!" Mr. Caeser said. Then he stood and came around the back of my chair, where he placed his strong hands on my shoulders as if he were sponsoring me into some secret society. "What we have here is pure and simple honesty, a rare—the rarest— of human qualities. He does not answer because he does not know, and this from one semantically talented. Do you have any idea how rare this reaction is in Caeser family annals? We are used to people telling us exactly what we want to hear. We are never disagreed with, even on those occasions when we know ourselves to be wrong! Oh, this one's a treasure, Justin; you've done well."

Mr. Caeser resumed his place at the head of the table. He stood, glass in hand. "A toast to this rare find. May he find happiness in our midst. May our home be his."

"And may he never leave us," Mrs. Caeser said.

TEN

I have no idea who helped me up the stairs, got me out of my clothes and into monogrammed pajamas, and even tucked me into bed. I slept in a drunken stupor, dreaming about a Phi Beta Kappa key swinging like a pendulum, hitting me in the face, nicking me with tiny cuts no matter how hard I tried to move my head out of the way. As happens in dreams, I could not move, and when I held my hands to my face, they came away filled with my blood. I bolted upright in the bed, examining my hands in the darkness.

Outside my window, sleet fell, the wind moaned, and the ocean came calling on the shore. I glanced at my wristwatch; it was 2 A.M.

On shaky legs, I stood and flicked on a small lamp next to my bed. I sat back down and tried to clear my head. I was dizzy and, as always, felt so stupid for allowing myself to get drunk. My mother shook her head and the smoke from my father's pipe thickened behind his *Wall Street Journal*.

What did I recall of the evening? Toasts, champagne, wine. It was a bit much and I rushed to the bathroom as my stomach telegraphed my brain: Get rid of the stuff! Now! I heaved into the commode and choked out an oath: Never, never again. I looked at myself in the mirror and was overwhelmed with self-pity. I could have cried. For myself, of course.

And then . . . then I heard something, or maybe I didn't. Maybe it was a feeling, the movement of air, the softest swishing sound, someone or something was gliding past my door. Soft, effortless motion. I returned to my bed, flicked the lamp off, and plunged my world into black.

Even with a monstrous hangover, even in the most dire circumstances, we remain what we basically are. And I, God help me, am curious. I can't help it! I have this need to know everything. Even when I know pain is attached, I've got to know it all. Like when I go to the dentist, I've got to ask questions about every instrument on the tray. I want to know what will probe, what will stick, what will drill? My father says I would be a good FBI agent. I've always been that way. It made me a voracious reader and even something of a bore. My classmates called me "Mr. Ask," and I drove some of my teachers to distraction. That's what they said.

So I pushed my way up from the bed and tiptoed to my door.

As quietly as possible, with hands that shook from my excess, I turned the handle and the door opened sound-lessly. Before me was the dark and endless hall, which re-sembled an airport runway. Below, I had a sense of light, so I crept into the hall and then to the head of the stairs and with a deep breath looked down, down, down into the entrance hall.

And saw a ghost.

The mind can be so kind an ally. I immediately thought, Fool, you're still drunk. I squeezed my eyes shut and then opened them, certain that my apparition would have van-ished.

It was still there, moving about the hall, arms out-stretched almost in supplication and seemingly dancing to a music that I could not hear.

It was, as ghost are, white, all white, with long white hair trailing down its back. Then it turned and seemed to look up the stairs at me, black holes where eyes should have been.

I then went through my first such experience with mor-tal terror, whirling about and racing back up the hall to my room, where I fumbled at the door, finally flung it open, slammed it behind me, collapsed on the bed, fought to get under the covers, which I pulled up over my head, and lay there trembling. My heart tried to beat its way out of my rib cage and breath came from me in great gasps, as if I had been pulled half-drowned from the water.

I awoke with fists shut tight and a terrible ache in my jaw. I must have slept with my teeth clenched in fear. I was still afraid and it was broad daylight. I was afraid and that's not like me. I do not believe in seances, Ouija boards, apparitions, visions, or any other unproven myths that are fun on "Twilight Zone" but have no place in real life.

All of this I told myself, but I took little comfort from my philosophy and words. Despite the alcohol I had consumed, I had seen something.

Should I tell Justin? I considered it. I needed to unload my experience into someone's ears. The day before, I absolutely would have done so. He was my friend, my colleague; I could tell him anything. But a day is a long time and I must admit I was no longer quite so sure. About what? About anything. These bizarre people had disoriented me; I was a Boy Scout who had lost his compass.

The Caesers' attitudes and reactions were so distant from anything I had ever known that I hesitated telling them anything. They had lost contact with me. I no longer completely trusted them and could not have said why.

I also suspected that if necessary, they would lie.

E L E V E N

I ate breakfast alone—a marvelous porridge, huckleberry pancakes, and eggs. Kingsley acknowledged—but only grudgingly and with eyes downcast, as if he was confessing to a murder—that the family dined only in the evening.

At the head of the breakfast table, I felt like Nero and filled my gullet accordingly. A door opened and Justin bounded in, full of energy, enthusiasm, and compliments. "My family, you wowed them, they love you!"

"They do?" I asked, mouth full of food, more at the ready on the end of my fork.

He studied me. I could see a question written on his face and that he was struggling with just how to ask it. "And you? What do you think of the Caesers?"

"Charming. And different. I've never known anyone like you."

"I warned you," he said with a nervous grin.

"You sure did."

"Unpleasantly so? Be frank," he said.

"No, no. Just, well, different."

"You know you're a funny fellow yourself. You ask one million questions but resist answering them yourself." Now there was mild irritation on his face and I had the feeling he wished I would choke on the porridge, which I could not stop eating.

"All right. The Caesers are fabulous!"

"Meaning?" he asked.

"Hey, what are we playing? Twenty Questions?"

"Yes. A game no doubt created by one Marion Anderson."

I put my fork down, stopped chewing. "Justin, you've got to understand, surely you do, that I've never known people so wealthy. It's a bit awesome."

"And what else?"

"Well, outspoken. You don't refrain from anything."

He smiled broadly, big teeth jutting over that pendulous pink bottom lip. "We don't have to."

"Hey, give me time. I'll come up with a complete analysis, I promise," I said lightly.

His face clouded. "Oh, I don't believe it's necessary that you go that far."

Why did I have the feeling that I had been warned?

"You've got my word," I said.

"Well then, come on. I'll show you our workplace."

"Sounds right out of Dickens," I said.

I followed him into "our workplace," the music room. This miniature palace was in gold and white, the woodwork overlaid in gold and silver. "Come on," he said, "I'll give you the grand tour. That's a musical clock made by one Charles Clay in London in 1736. We keep it in here because when it chimes, the bells play operatic arias. Had to have it rewired of course. Handel owned that harpsichord and Haydn used it. The English harp is from 1850 and God only knows how old the organ is. My sister could tell you, she's the artist in the family."

I assumed he meant Eleanor.

"And this," he said standing at a Steinway, "this is my baby. It was decorated in Paris and my father presented it to me on my tenth birthday, when I had evidenced some musical talent. And there you have it, that'll be fifty cents, tips not only accepted but anticipated."

"It's, it's intimidating. I hope I can work here," I said, drinking in all that gold and silver.

He slapped my back. "Not to worry! Of course you can. It's just a room, just an empty room really. It's us who'll make it come alive. We'll do great things here. I have every confidence. Don't you? Honestly, don't you?"

"I feel very small and very hung over."

"Take a walk; walk on the beach or in the gardens. Clear your head. I want to get started. That melody that's given me so much trouble, well, I believe I've got it, or just about have it. About an hour? We'll meet right here in an hour. You'll love the walled gardens, designed, I may have mentioned, by Frederick Law Olmsted, the same man who—"

"Planned Central Park," I said.

"Sorry. I forgot."

I returned to my room and put on a heavy jacket and gloves. The temperature was dropping and by late afternoon it would be at the freezing point. The dead of winter was only a breath away.

Kingsley directed me to a narrow stone path with guide wires along either side that led to the sandy beach, a long crescent with promontories at each end. Far out, I could see brightly painted lobster markers and overhead were screaming gulls and herons swooping and wheeling above the turbulent water. The surf boomed in my ears and the cold air cleared my head as promised.

Ahead, I saw someone walking, hands gesturing, having a conversation with himself.

It was Timothy, bundled up in a khaki greatcoat, with a green Tyrolean hat clamped down on his head as if it had been shoved there. I cupped my hands and called his name, but in the wind he didn't hear me. I did it again and he stopped, whirled about like God had spoken. As I approached, he squinted to determine just who it was on that cold and blustery beach.

"Have they sent you for me?" There was excitement in his question and spittle flew from his mouth.

"Sent me? No. I'm just walking. Bit of a hangover."

"I thought they'd sent you. 'Go fetch Timothy.' As in 'Go fetch Fido.' They tend to think of others that way. Can't help it, I guess. The way it's always been. That, of course, excuses everything. What's your name? Should I remember?"

"No reason. Anderson."

"First or last?"

"Last. First is Marion with an *o*. My mother loved Marian Anderson."

He had no idea about whom I was talking. "Well, good for her. I guess. I have no idea who my mother loved, my father, perhaps."

I laughed. That was the best response I had ever received to my inane but oft-repeated explanation. As always, I thanked God my mother had not loved ZaSu Pitts.

"Have they told you they loved you yet?" he asked suddenly, his dimples exact commas in his face.

"Huh? Oh, them!"

"Yes. Them," he said, and hugged himself against the cold as we both ducked at a low-flying heron sweeping over us with a shriek. "Well, have they?"

"As a matter of fact, they have. Or at least Justin has."

"They love me, too," he said so solemnly that I had to smother laughter. "And what do you think of them, Mr. Marion Anderson? Have you come to love them yet, or are you slow to love?" he asked.

"You sound like Ann Landers," I said. His abstract conversation was beginning to get to me, as were the cold and the wind.

"Sorry. It's the lawyer in me. Do you?"

"Can't say. I don't know how I feel about people I just met. Except astonished. They are astonishing. I guess all that wealth . . ."

Timothy snorted, causing him to resemble a pink frog. "I've known many people with wealth. Went to school with one of the Rockefellers, stayed in his home on several weekends. Do believe me, in fact you'd better believe me, I've never known anyone like, like . . ."

He was having trouble saying their name. I said, "The Caesers."

He nodded, clapping his hands for warmth.

"Actually, I got too drunk to form a reliable opinion and even had I been sober, it's a little early to really know them. But I will. I'm a student of people," I said.

"Better hurry," I thought I heard him mutter.

I said, "I beg your pardon?"

Timothy shook his head, mouth pressed tight, and said, "Nothing."

We walked in silence and listened to the ocean, which was gray and loud, giving off a hissing sound, as if it were boiling. He stopped and grabbed my arm. "You seem like a nice enough young fellow." We had come to some lichen-covered rocks, near them the dead remnants of wild roses and bayberry. I saw a redwing blackbird and a couple of bobolinks. They all seemed lost.

We sat on some white rocks and stared out at the ocean. He could have been discussing the lobster markers, so quietly did he speak. "Leave here now. Don't even pack. Leave."

I sighed. "Timothy, I don't know what's bugging you, but believe me, I'm no competitor of yours for anything that the Caesers have. I've come here to work, that's it, plain and simple work. And when I'm finished . . ."

"Oh to be sure, when you're finished. My God, you sound like I did! First the luxury, the indescribable luxury, the every wish, the every whim at your fingertips, at the ready, it's intoxicating, all velvet and incense. It gets to a fellow," he said, and then added sadly, "It got to me."

"You're the only person I ever met who hit the jackpot and seems down about it," I said.

"The Caesers love me, Eleanor loves me," he said, then buried his head in his hands and groaned, "Oh God, oh my God, oh God help me."

I lewdly thought, Wow! She must be something!

He looked up at me with rheumy eyes; they seemed faded. "And what do you think of my Eleanor?" He said *my* without a possessive inflection, as if it were her first name.

"She's the most beautiful woman I've ever seen," I said honestly.

"Go on," he urged.

I thought, And obviously the hottest. But I didn't talk that way, not out loud, and besides, she was his fiancée. "I understand she's an artist."

"No doubt she'll paint you." This he said with dread, which I interpreted as jealousy. I couldn't blame him.

"She's painted me," he said. "Only the face is lacking."

"No face?" I asked.

"She's waiting," he said, and I debated pressing on. As usual, my curiosity won out.

"Waiting? For what?"

He smiled a clown's smile, someplace between mirth and overwhelming sorrow. "The right moment. When? Only Eleanor knows that."

"You know you sound a little like the Caesers, all those hints, everything behind a gauze curtain. It's beginning to bug me!"

"I'm sorry, truly I am. It's just that . . ." His voice drifted off in the wind, which now was howling.

"If you've got something to say, say it!"

"By all means, say it. And how, may I ask, do I know if I can trust you?" he asked.

"I am a very trustworthy man," I said.

He peered at me as though an examination might prove or disprove my claim. "Let me sleep on it."

"Sure. Sleep on it," I said, standing and stamping my feet to get some feeling back in them.

He tugged at my jacket. "Don't take my words so lightly, Mr. Marion Anderson. We are talking here about a matter of life and death. Mine for certain and, just possibly, yours."

I believed him. A gull cried as if it had overheard us and believed him, too.

He looked about uneasily, took a deep breath, and said, "I'll meet you right here tomorrow. The same time."

"Why not now?"

He stood. "She'll need me. Before she sleeps, after she sleeps, before and after dinner, before she paints, and after." There was no bragging in his voice.

I blurted out, "You must be one hell of a man, Timothy!"

"No. Not at all. It's the food, the food they feed you. All laced with aphrodisiacs. We are all studs here."

TWELVE

Justin and I put in four solid hours of productive work. The weird events of the past hours didn't seem to affect either my concentration or my creative juices. Even Justin noticed. "You're cooking!" he said. I believe the work was a necessary release valve; my system appreciated it and responded accordingly. For those four hours, the Caeser family and Timothy's behavior were forgotten.

The only interruption—and a most welcome one—was Kingsley with my lunch: cold lobster and a chilled bottle of Clos des Mouches. Justin, who naturally wouldn't eat until dinner, smiled like a parent at my wolfish excess. "I think you're getting as much pleasure out of this lobster as I am," I said.

"It's Mother," he said, "insists we've got to put some weight on you."

"Why do mothers want everyone fat?" I asked, toasting all mothers with my wine, which was chilled to perfection. My mother, my father, their world, which used to be my world, seemed light-years away, on some other planet, another time. The rich are not only different, they restructure those they touch into someone different. Marion Anderson was not the same man he had been. I wondered whether I liked the new me?

Justin smiled as though he could read my thoughts. "You are enjoying yourself here?"

"Now who wouldn't?" I asked, putting my glass down as Kingsley mysteriously appeared for my tray.

"How'd Kingsley know when to come?" I asked.

He pointed down. "There's a button right here under the rug."

"Is there anything you all don't possess?" It was overwhelming.

Justin's face clouded over, as if gray sun motes had drifted across his pink complexion. "Nothing is perfect."

"Bah, humbug!" I said.

"Nothing is perfect."

"Want to be specific? What's missing in paradise?"

He smiled patiently. "Very important things." Then he clapped his hands, dismissing the subject. "Not to worry! They're being tended to." The cloud lifted.

"Justin, why do I get the feeling that you're teasing me . . . no, that's not the word. Those hints you keep dropping, are they a dare for me to intellectually solve or are they . . ."

"Sorry. I'm used to talking with only members of my own family and naturally, with each other, we don't have to go into a lot of detail. I must be erroneously doing the same with you. It's probably terribly annoying. I'll try to watch it. On the other hand . . ."

"Ah!" I said. "On the other hand . . ."

"Maybe you're seeing the real me. Maybe I have a need to be elusive, mysterious even. I can't imagine why, not with you. I trust you. I can, can't I?"

"Of course," I said. "I don't want your body or your money. Just your music!"

We laughed and even as we did, I broke all vows. "Er, Justin, there is one thing . . ."

He stopped laughing so suddenly that I wondered whether it had been genuine. "Yes?" he asked solemnly.

"Last night, or rather, early this morning, something happened."

He smiled broadly. "You awoke with an erection. First in years."

"I heard something."

"This is a huge home. Some of it creaks. And then there's the wind and the ocean below. You have noticed them?" he said.

"Yeah, but then I went out into the hall and I saw something."

He waited.

"It was a ghost."

He threw back his head and emitted a roar of laughter. "You drunk bastard, you!"

I laughed weakly. "Yeah, I know, but really I don't. I really did see one. A ghost."

"Booo!" he said through cupped fists.

"A female ghost . . ."

"Naturally," he said derisively.

"It, she . . . was down the hall. Dancing." I felt foolish. Very foolish.

He ripped off a perfect, delightful melody, all wispy and gossamer and dancing. "The dancing ghost, booo booo!"

"Forget it. I was drunk," I said. Now I had doubts.

"Yes. Forget it."

THIRTEEN

Dinner was different. More different. Tension was in the air, and there was Eleanor. I could not take my eyes away. She wore a sexy version of a man's tuxedo with the cummerbund worn outside the jacket. It was hot pink and tight. Her matching bow tie was that same startling color. She wore no shirt. Her hair was pulled back and braided in a complicated large bun, with black, silver, and hot pink ribbons braided in the coif. She wore hot pink lipstick and a large diamond man's lapel pin. There were gloves with the fingers pointing up inside her breast pocket.

I looked around the table at the Caesers through different, more questioning eyes. The warnings I had received from Johnny Atooza in the village and then from Timothy forced me to examine more acutely these exotic birds in whose midst I found myself. They were a handsome people and in some indefinable way resembled each other. Yet they didn't. Mr. Caeser was huge, Mrs. Caeser tiny and dark. Still . . .

That they were eccentric, there was no doubt. People neither act nor speak like the Caesers. But then people, the rest of us, have to edit, censor both our speech and our actions; none of us can afford the consequences of an ill-taken step. However, that was not a factor with the Caesers. Their money crossed out consequences. It occurred to me that for all that wealth, they were a likable and gracious people, and I decided that Johnny Atooza was probably attempting to hurt them for some long-ago ill he felt they had committed against him or someone in his family.

However, Timothy presented different problems. Why would he, soon to be by marriage a member of that family, warn me so dramatically against them? Unless he thought I might have a yen for Eleanor. Or she for me? Was it pure jealousy?

I looked at her. She was radiant and I swallowed nervously. Mr. Caeser looked at her and then at me and winked, like Santa before going up a chimney. I smiled at him.

We ate, or I should say, *I* ate fish, all kinds of fish, from lobster chowder to fried haddock, pollack, scrod, flounder, sole, trout, cod, and bass. It was called, I believe—at a restaurant where my mother, father, and I ate every Sunday after church—a fisherman's delight.

I alone seemed to enjoy it as the family quietly picked at it with little attempt at conversation. They didn't seem to be the same people they'd been the night before. Mr. and Mrs. Caeser cast glances at each other and then heavenward, as though seeking divine inspiration or intervention. I did not know their needs.

"Look at him," Eleanor said, pointing my way with a fork, an empty one. There was incredulity in her voice. "He likes it."

Sounding very maternal, Mrs. Caeser said, "Let him eat, let him eat."

Timothy, head low over a third plate of chowder, said, "By all means, let him eat." Then he laughed as though he had told a joke. No one joined in.

"Stop it," said Justin. "Let him enjoy it." Even as he spoke, he pushed his plate away in what looked like disgust.

"Eat!" roared Mr. Caeser and I began to chew faster.

Kingsley entered, leaned down, and whispered to Mr. Caeser, who slammed a meaty fist on the table. "That's more like it!" He beamed. "Send him in, send him in." Then he announced to the table, "Mr. Kalil is here."

I felt certain they would break out in applause, so brightened did the mood suddenly become.

Mr. Kalil was unique, even among this odd bunch.

He was a dour, dark-skinned man who wore a red fez and a tiny red bow tie. There was an ugly scar on his face, extending from his right cheek all the way down his throat. It had not been stitched up very well. He bowed, or tried to, as Mr. Caeser stood and enveloped him in his arms.

"How stands our oracle from the Mideast?" Mr. Caeser asked, holding the man's face in his hands as if he were going to give him a couple of those diplomatic kisses the Russians are always trading.

"Very poorly, I'm afraid," Mr. Kalil whined, and I thought I heard some New York mixed in with the exotic East.

Mr. Caeser actually stumbled backward as if shot in the heart. "What? What's that you say?"

"Trouble," Mr. Kalil said, only it sounded like "twouble."

"Oh? What kind of trouble? I don't purchase trouble. Millions do not purchase trouble!" Mr. Caeser said.

"I am in personal trouble," Mr. Kalil said sadly. He looked like a Shriner who had gotten rained on.

Mr. Caeser lost all control and began shaking the smaller man. Never was Mr. Caeser's strength more evident. It looked as if Mr. Kalil would break in two, head going one way, the rest of him the other. "Goddamn you, I am not paying for excuses!" Mr. Caeser roared.

Mrs. Caeser smiled sweetly and said softly, "Dear, our guest."

Mr. Caeser let the poor man go, made a half-apologetic bow in my direction, and instructed Mr. Kalil, "You come with me."

We watched them depart, Kalil in the lead, like a tiny tug leading a giant liner.

"What in the shit is going on?" Eleanor said.

Timothy said, "Dearest, your language."

She screeched into his white face: "Oh, shut up! You think he's never heard *shit*?"

Timothy resumed eating his chowder and drinking one more glass of wine. It must have been his twentieth.

Justin said, "Take it easy. Father'll straighten it all out."

Mrs. Caeser said with a bitter, wintery smile, "Well, we certainly do hope so, don't we?" She looked right at her daughter, who looked at Timothy as though seeing him for the first time that evening. Then the two women traded smiles.

All attempts at conversation ceased. We sat there just as Kingsley entered and made one of his royal pronouncements. "Mr. Caeser would like the family to assemble in the library in ten minutes."

They didn't fool around. It was as if a starter's pistol had sounded before the race, and in a moment, Timothy and I sat there alone. He was not in good shape. He had eaten and drunk himself into the prelims of a big-time stupor. He was twisting his napkin as if it were a tourniquet and he was biting away at his chubby cheeks from the inside. It occurred to me that Timothy was terrified and I became frightened for him and for myself.

I poured him a glass from the magic decanter. It was the first time I had ever held it and I let my fingers play over its remarkable surface and the serpent that formed its handle.

Timothy was shaking so badly that he couldn't get his glass to his mouth and I had to help him. He gulped away, looking up at me with watery eyes and showing appreciation with a nod that spilled some of the wine down his chin. I hit him on the back and he successfully got it down.

I sat down next to him. He tied his handkerchief into a knot and was pulling at the ends as if he were performing an unsuccessful parlor trick.

"Timothy, you've got to tell me what's going on here."

He made some kind of squawking sound and said something incomprehensible.

I squeezed his hand between mine and tried to give him the strength that he so desperately needed. "Come on, Timothy, you can do it," I said, wondering, Do what?

He nodded, tried to focus on me, and whispered, "Not here."

"In the morning? Remember? You said in the morning."

He blinked as if he was standing in a spotlight. "I don't now about the morning. I just don't know."

"Timothy, what are we talking about?" I felt like Abbott and Costello. "Timothy, who's on first?"

I felt lousy because big tears were streaming down his face, though he made no sound. "Aw, stop, Timothy. It can't be that bad."

"It is the worst. Think the worst and it's worse than that," he said, making no effort to wipe his eyes. I did with the napkin. He just sat there.

"Do you need help? Because if you do, I'll help," I said. I felt so sorry for the guy but didn't know why.

"You would? You'd help me? You don't even know me. I was a damn fine lawyer. I'm published, extensively published!"

"I don't doubt it. I can tell."

"Please don't patronize me," he said.

"I'm sorry. Forgiven? Look man, you've got to tell me." I realized I was squeezing his hand. I let go.

He sighed and for a moment I was afraid he'd start bawling again. "Yes. It's the only way. The only chance. You do understand, don't you?"

"Damn right!" I lied. I didn't understand any of it, but I had the feeling I'd better.

"Tonight, after she goes to sleep, I'll go to your room. I'll tell you everything, and we'll make plans!" He sounded like a child and I wondered whether he was in shock.

"I'll be waiting," I said.

Timothy crept to the door, turned, and held a finger to his lips. "Shhh," he said.

I decided to get some fresh air.

FOURTEEN

The house seemed empty, even the ever-present Kingsley was no place in sight. I started to go to my room to get my coat but decided not to; I would only go out long enough for fresh air, away from the tension and the sick behavior of Timothy.

It was freezing and I felt as if I was wearing nothing but

a handkerchief. I turned about and looked at that Taj Mahal—that's what it was like—and shook my head that human beings could dwell in such splendor. I wondered whether I could get a photo of it to send my folks. What would they say? Their son, their only son, dwelling in a fairy-tale castle? My mother would flip. She was the dreamer. It was from her that I had gotten my dreams, my dreams that seemed miraculously likely to come true. I was overwhelmed with excitement and wanted to burst out in song: "If they could see me now." Then I thought of my father, who no doubt would speculate whether that splendor was paid for and whether I, in its golden midst, would make a fool of myself? I stuck my tongue out at him in the darkness.

In front of the house was a red Corvette that I hadn't noticed before. I peered in. Its rear compartment was filled with trunks, and the door on the driver's side was dented and beginning to rust. It had a New York license plate. Was it Mr. Kalil's?

The house was surrounded by tall shrubs and I found myself peering between them and looking into huge picture windows at what was obviously the library. Like everything else that had to do with the Caesers, its size was epic. There was book after book bound in gold, and even a spiral staircase going up to a second tier.

Behind a massive desk—but he would require one—was Mr. Caeser, legs outstretched, tie hanging loose from his collar. His hands were wrapped about his big stomach. His face was expressionless.

His family sat before him, rigid in straight-backed chairs, like students before the headmaster. Off to the side sat Mr. Kalil, slumped over as if he had cramps, fezzed head buried in his hands. He had several of what looked like diamond rings on his hands and a huge gold I.D. bracelet on his wrist, and his cuffs were frayed!

It was like watching a movie—a silent one. I could hear nothing.

There are a handful of moments in life when the startling realization hits us that we must make a choice, a decision, and that there is no time—as we have been taught—to think it out, no time to apply logic or even experience. We're there and it—a moment—is there. And we take a momentous step and never in our lives are we at all certain why we did.

Standing there in the night, the thought came to me without prelude that this was such a moment. I could stay back and watch but never know what was happening in that library or I could take three steps forward through the shrubbery, press myself into the darkness, and listen. And know.

Did I want to know? It was none of my business and I was these people's guest, eating their food, sharing their home and their company. The gentleman in me said no, but it said it very softly. Drowning it out were the voices of Johnny Atooza and Timothy. In my life, I had never been warned of anything. My parents were not warners. My teachers had chosen some other method. No one had ever said, If you don't study you, won't make the dean's list. Now, in the course of a few days, I had received not one but two warnings, and both had mentioned my safety as being involved.

I took those three steps forward and found that now I could not only see but hear.

Mr. Caeser was speaking in quite natural conversational tones. "Are you quite certain? Are your processes intact? We are quite aware of your little predilections," he said, then touched his nose and sniffed.

Mr. Kalil jumped to his feet. "For God's sake, do you think I've got brain damage, that I'm imagining?" He sat back down. "Oh, that I were."

"Be quiet, be quiet, I say. I will brook no shouting in

this house!" Mr. Caeser shouted, causing the hapless Kalil to collapse back into his own comforting arms. "Well?" Mr. Caeser asked, more calmly.

Kalil spoke. "Mr. Caeser, honorable sir—"

"Oh, get on with it," Eleanor said. Her foot stirred, as if she wanted to give Mr. Kalil a swift kick in the posterior.

"Have I ever failed the Caesers? Ever?" Kalil asked.

Mr. Caeser gave an imperial nod, but just barely.

"I, Kalil, like my father before and his father before him, have furnished the noble Caesers only the finest. In this very room, you have often referred to me as an artist. It was you who gave me these precious rings"—here he moved his fingers like goldfish as all his jewelry gave off little sparks—"as a token of your esteem." His fingers were manicured. "I tell you, honorable sir, the police have taken an interest in Kalil. Not the local police, whom, I say in all modesty, I own. Do you know what they call me? Little father." He smiled grimly and shook his head in memory. "But Interpol is another matter. I do not own Interpol. Not even the Caesers own Interpol. And it is neither my imagination—which you know to be glorious—nor my little . . . pastime that has caused me to see what is not present or to hear that which I do not hear."

"What does he hear?" Mrs. Caeser asked her husband.

Mr. Caeser looked at her and then at Kalil. "Yes. What do you hear?"

"Funny sounds on my telephone. Clicks and once a squeak." He made the sound. It was suitably electronic.

"Tapped."

Mr. Kalil nodded eagerly. "Of course, tapped. Not that that causes me alarm. I say nothing on the telephone."

"He's called this house," Justin said. He sounded as frightened as Mr. Kalil.

Eleanor said, "What a fucking mess."

"Of course I called here. And why not? I am an international wine dealer and the Caesers have one of the great cellars on earth," Mr. Kalil said.

"What are your plans, Kalil?" Mr. Caeser asked.

"I drive to Boston tonight. Tomorrow, I leave for Brazil. For the time being, America has seen the last of Ibrahim Kalil." He said it as if the loss was America's.

"Suppose they stop you?" Justin said. He sounded like a district attorney. "Suppose there's an all-points bulletin out for you at this very moment. Suppose you get to the airport and someone says, Would you step this way for a moment?"

"It won't happen!" Mr. Kalil said, wringing his hands.

"But suppose it does?" Mrs. Caeser asked. She looked like an evil gypsy casting a spell.

"You would talk," Mr. Caeser said. He sounded confident.

"Perhaps Mr. Kalil should get on his way," Mrs. Caeser said, sounding like a gracious hostess.

The family mulled that over, looking at one another. It was as if Mr. Kalil wasn't even among them.

"Yes, on his way," Eleanor said with a throaty chuckle.

"Why wait?" asked Justin.

"You can tell he's in a hurry," Mrs. Caeser said. She sounded maternal.

Mr. Kalil smiled at each of them, as if he was responding to separate jokes. It made the scar on his face jut out. "I thought you ladies and gentlemen might arrive at just such a conclusion. So logical. And practical. I have taken some precautions against just such an eventuality. My attorney has a letter to turn over to Interpol if he cannot reach me in Brazil in two days."

"Two days," Mr. Caeser said.

"We were just kidding," Eleanor said.

"Can't you take a joke?" Mrs. Caeser asked lightly.

Mr. Kalil said, "A joke. Of course." He stood, straightened his fez. "And now, ladies and gentlemen, I, Kalil, bid you a most pleasant good evening. And *bon appetit,* by all means that." He bowed and headed for the door.

Mrs. Caeser called, "Good trip, Mr. Kalil."

The front door opened and Kingsley and Mr. Kalil stood in the light. Mr. Kalil proceeded to his Corvette and drove off down the mountain. Kingsley stood about, as if he was sniffing the night air, and I pressed farther into the shadows.

"What a sleaze," Eleanor said.

"What a problem," Justin said.

"What are we going to do?" Mrs. Caeser asked.

Mr. Caeser pushed his girth upright, stretched, and said, "I'll sleep on it."

Eleanor began laughing. The others stared incredulously at her.

"Pray share your mirth, Eleanor. We could all use some," Mr. Caeser said.

"You'll sleep on it, I'll sleep with it," she said.

For a moment, they didn't get it, then they did and joined in ugly laughter and even embraced one another, and I got out of there fast.

FIFTEEN

I undressed, put on my pajamas, and sat upright in bed. Would Timothy come? The room was pitch-dark and my mind was racing as I tried to assimilate what I had overheard from that meeting in the library.

I arrived at a few conclusions. Mr. Kalil had performed for years some kind of unscrupulous service for the family.

I had a feeling it had to do with big-time narcotics. I couldn't imagine what else. Heroin? A particulary big and remunerative shipment?

Mr. Kalil's warning to the family about his arrangements with his lawyer didn't surprise me. I was positive that this family would do anything and never give their acts a second thought. That Kalil had to take these precautions indicated that the family had done ugly things before. I wondered whether they'd go as far as murder. Yeah, they would, I decided. Once again, death had been thrust into my world and I had the distressing feeling that death was a mobile circle, moving in on me.

Mr. Kalil's departure had left the family in some kind of need, something to which they had to give some thought. But what? The narcotics, the wealth that would continue to accrue to the family from drugs—was it that important? Were they that greedy? Insatiable people who never got enough? That didn't shock me. Every day the newspapers were filled with millionaires, Wall Street insiders, defense contractors who had been greedy.

I must have sat there for an hour when I felt a stirring outside my door and a gust of air told me the door had been opened and someone was entering my room. I could see its shadow now moving toward my bed and I whispered, "Timothy, thank goodness. Come on in."

No answer. "Come on, Timothy, cut it out. I've had it for today."

Then it occurred to me it wasn't Timothy and I sagged back and tried to say something wise or angry, but nothing came out. It just didn't come out because my vocal cords froze in fear and I felt spittle trickle out the corner of my mouth and traverse my chin.

I closed my eyes, breathed deeply, and tried to pull myself together. I could hear the other thing breathing softly and I said to myself, Fool, it's just another person, someone like you, and once again I started breathing normally.

"I'm going to turn on the light," I said.

"Don't!" a female voice begged.

I lay back down. The next move was up to her and I thought I knew who *her* was.

"Are you afraid?" she asked. I thought I knew that voice.

"Eleanor," I said. Now I wasn't so sure, however. It was her, yet it wasn't. The voice was the same but—

"You should be afraid, very afraid." Oh Christ, I thought, another warning. Really a bit much. I was warned out.

"Who are you?" I asked, irritated.

"Annabel. As who lives 'in a kingdom by the sea.'"

"Annabel Lee," I said. I loved Edgar Allan Poe.

"Annabelle Caeser."

"The twin! I wondered . . ."

"Now you know."

"Annabel Lee"—and I would always call her that— "honestly, I don't know anything."

"Oh, of course. Only the Caesers know. It's a wonderful advantage."

"Advantage . . . the Caesers!" I announced, as if at a tennis match.

She giggled. She was a child-woman and she was in the darkness.

"Please, may I turn on this light?"

"No, I'll go away. In the light, I'll melt like an ice, a lemon ice in the heat. We have a machine that makes them. They are so delicious. My father makes them for me. But you can't eat them in the winter."

"No."

"I should go. Should I go?"

"No."

"You thought I was Timothy. Poor Timothy."

"Why? Why *poor* Timothy?"

71

"He drinks too much. I think Timothy is an alcoholic. Isn't that sad?"

I reached out and caught her wrist. "I don't believe you. He drinks, sure, but there's more. The guy is dying of fright!"

"You're hurting me," she said, but made no move to escape.

My face was in hers. Her breath smelled like a delightful purple mint I used to love as a child. "Tell me what's going on or I'll turn on this light!"

"No," she wailed, but I did.

Annabel Lee was the identical copy of her sister except that she was white, all white. Annabel Lee was an albino.

I flicked off the light. There wasn't a whole lot to say. "I'm sorry."

"You are a cruel man," she said.

"No, please don't feel that way. It's this feeling I'm getting, I don't like it. Worse, I don't know what to do with it. I don't even know why I'm feeling this way."

"What feeling?"

"Well, it's going to sound, I don't know, silly! I mean I feel silly saying it. I feel desperate," I said, then realized I was still holding her wrist. I let go.

"Oh, I know that feeling. It's terrible. But I know why I feel that way," she said.

"Can we be friends?" I asked. I had the terrible need to have one. Somehow, Justin didn't qualify anymore.

"I've never had one," she said cautiously, as if there was inherent danger.

"Let me be your friend," I said.

"In the darkness. It would have to be that way," she said.

"Okay, I accept. In the darkness."

"But can I trust you?" she asked. It was like dealing with a child, intriguing and at the same time irritating.

"I could ask you the same question. You are one of

them." Oh my God, what was I saying? "Hey look, I didn't mean . . ." I began.

"Turn on the light," she said, childishness vanished from her voice. I did.

"Not so bad, huh?" I was keeping pity out of my voice, but that's what I felt. She was a perfect sketch of her sister, one done on a white canvas.

"Am I repulsive? I've always wanted to ask somebody that. Somebody who would tell me the truth without being cruel," she said.

"You are different," I replied.

"Yes?"

"But also beautiful or maybe that's not the word. Exotic. Like one of those Siberian tigers in a zoo," I said.

She chuckled exactly as her sister did. "I am in a zoo, but I put myself there."

I squeezed her hand in reply.

"You're my first. I've never held hands with a man. I suppose because we're becoming friends it's all right," she said.

"Friends do sometimes hold hands. Now Annabel Lee, I've got to ask you, why the warning?"

She smiled. "Oh that. For effect. To make an impression. It's not easy in the dark, you know."

"You're certain that was all, for effect?"

"Silly! Of course. Now I must go," she said.

"When will I see you again?"

"I'll come back when everyone has gone to sleep. I'll be your night friend. Like a hoot owl," she said.

She was at the door. "Annabel Lee, one question please."

"One."

"Have you ever been outside? Ever?"

"When I was a baby, I was taken to physicians all over the world. Since then, never."

SIXTEEN

In the morning, I awakened to a gloomy, dark world. The fog had rolled in with fury and made the day opaque.

I joined Justin in the music room. He was exquisitely dressed and groomed as usual, today in a brown tweed suit. There was one difference. On his right cheek was a narrow two-inch Band-Aid. He noted my attention.

"Clumsy me," he said, touching it. "I fell. Gave myself a good jolt."

"I didn't know rich people did things like that. I thought just klutzes."

"You mean like you," he said, and instantly he was playing something to which you could dance. I named it "The Waltz of the Klutzes" and it went into our show. So much for hours of toil and waiting for inspiration!

The work went well. Except for the wind and the ocean, we could have been on some other planet. The fog made it complete. We had the most perfect working conditions.

"Justin, where can I work on these lyrics? I need a desk."

"The library. There's a desk the size of an aircraft carrier. My father uses it sometimes because it's the only one that fits him, but usually it's not in use. Come on, I'll show you."

We entered that room, the size of a substantial church.

"There are twenty thousand volumes. That stained-glass window is from the clerestory of Salisbury Cathedral in England. Up that staircase is where the rare books are kept. There are original manuscripts by Shakespeare and

Chaucer and a Gutenberg Bible. Be careful going up the spiral; my sister fell there once, as a wee child," he said.

I wondered which sister but dared not ask him. I said, "Justin, is it okay if I walk about the grounds a bit? My mornings are so free."

"Silly goose! What a stupid question. Of course you can. Why must you be so damn melodramatic? You sound like the Prisoner of Zenda!"

I persisted. "Anyplace? Can I go anyplace?"

It irritated him and he fought not to show it, but his eyes narrowed into slits. "Are you a law-abiding citizen?"

"Sure. I'd say so."

"Well, when you come to a stop sign, stop. But you'd do that anyplace, wouldn't you?" he asked.

"I suppose so," I said.

"Just obey the law," he replied.

"Whose law?" I asked.

He smiled. "The Caesers', who else?"

Dinner was remarkable. Timothy was not with us, nor did anyone explain his absence. Eleanor was spectacular, and if she missed her fiancé, it was not evident. In fact, I found myself seated next to her and she literally lavished her attention on me.

I did not detect that the Caesers minded one bit. It was as if they expect it, even desired it! Her strapless gown was skintight, with sequins sewn into a gold and black leopard-skin pattern. She wore a miniscule cloche on her head, fashioned of tiny gold beads. Her eye shadow was metallic gold and there was a thick gold bracelet around her arm, between shoulder and elbow.

The meal was an old-fashioned Indian clambake, Caeser style. There were fresh clams with corn and potatoes covered with layers of seaweed that had been soaked in salty seawater. Then the servants had wrapped this mixture up and cooked it over a charcoal fire built with rocks on the beach.

The red burgundy wine was a 1959 LaTache and it tasted like velvet.

Naturally, Mr. Caeser, stabbing at a clam without enthusiasm, dominated our talk. "Poor man," he said. Was he talking about me? I certainly fit the description. "He waits for lightning, for rain, and then for a rainbow. That it never comes doesn't disturb him for longer than a moment. He is a believer in: everything will be just fine; or, if you will, if you wait long enough, it will come; or tomorrow will be a better day!"

The big hand came slamming down on the table, causing everything including me to jump as if I'd been goosed. Even Kingsley paused, the decanter at the ready in his gloved fist.

Mr. Caeser, having made his exclamation point, continued his discourse. "But, by God, not the Caesers, not this family. We do not wait. We act! We are not supernumeraries in life's insignificant playlet. We command center stage; we demand it!" Then his voice grew intimate; a secret was being shared. "We do what we must. What pleases us." He looked in triumph about the table. His great chest heaved with emotion and I was afraid he'd have a stroke in the seaweed. "And you, sir?"

I was concentrating on chewing some seaweed, which I am not at all certain is meant to be chewed, when I realized he was addressing me. I swallowed. He extended a pudgy finger in my direction and I tried to meet his eyes but wasn't up to it. "Will you be a bit player? Come, sir, surely you've wondered? You're a talented man, a thinking creature; surely your destiny causes you some interest. In the dark of night, have you not wondered?"

"About me? Me! Yes, certainly. By all means!" What in God's name was I talking about? I hoped my weak answer might get me out of the way of that finger, which resembled a stunted blunderbuss.

"And?"

All of them were scrutinizing me as if man's fate hinged on my answer. The pressure was enormous. The seaweed tasted like burnt grass on my tongue and I cast a feverish glance at Justin, Help! He looked back at me with an expressionless face. As if he barely knew me, he studied me over the edge of his glass, like it was an optical instrument.

By my side, Eleanor stirred restlessly, her knee touching mine beneath the table, then moving away, as if I had a communicable disease.

Mrs. Caeser's eyes glowed with ferocious energy and she seemed to be reading my thoughts—of which I had none. That was the problem.

Mr. Caeser's finger was unbending, as if it had frozen there, and I wondered whether I was frozen in place also. "You will find in life, young man, there will be a moment, two at most, when destiny knocks. Fate. Rarely. Listen. Listen very carefully. What do you hear?"

I resisted their game. I did not want to enter their weird and somehow involving world any further. It was a golden quicksand. "I hear the wind. It's up tonight and I hear the ocean. It's raising hell on the beach."

"Listen!" he hissed. "Listen again, that wind, that ocean have always been here, will be here long after all of us are gone. But there is another sound. Your future knocking at the door. Answer it and tomorrow is yours. Whatever you want, whenever you want it. Can you even conceive of that? Remove all stupid impediments from your mind— money, time, limitations that send little men to the ground, defeated by time and all that they will never possess. But you! You reach out and it's there. Like those stupid pandas in the zoo. They eat their bamboo and, mysteriously, in the morning it's replenished as if it sprung up in the darkness. Imagine a world where the bamboo is always there! Can you?"

"It's very difficult," I said.

"I accept that," he said. "You've no North Star for gigantic dreams, no coordinates to plot by. This world, this world of limitless and unending possibilities, does it appeal to you? Come sir, does it appeal to you?"

I was human. "Of course."

He sighed. "That's a start."

Tension at the table let go like a marionette's strings released.

He reached inside his jacket pocket and removed a small box. "Come here, young man."

I stood on shaky legs and walked to the head of the table. It seemed like miles. "Extend your hand," he said. My hand was shaking and he stared at it with amusement. All the family was smiling. He opened the box and re-moved a magnificent opal ring set in thick gold and slipped it on my finger like a groom. His big paw was surprisingly soft, the skin slick. "A token of our burgeon-ing affection and interest."

Faust muttered thanks and slunk back to his seat. I felt unclean, as if I had been purchased and was no longer a free man. Nor did I have the courage to refuse the ring. I was confused, disoriented by his lecture.

Alice was deep in Wonderland.

In my room, I removed the ring, then rubbed at my finger where it had been. I held it up to the light from the table lamp and peered at it. I had never had anything that fine. A gift. Just a gift. What had I done to earn it? How had I so suddenly and so ostentatiously merited their affection? And what opportunity was knocking at my door? What had suddenly changed me in their eyes? I was certain there was a reason, a reason that mattered to the Caesers. I could no longer fathom their doing something just for the hell of it. I felt strange. My attitude toward them was rapidly changing. I wondered whether I should continue working with Justin. I didn't exactly feel the same about my friend.

Then I thought, Gut it out. Finish the show. You've started, now finish. After all, the Caesers were nothing to me. I had come into their lives, I would leave just as quickly and quietly. I could already envision the scene: I would wave and shout, Good-bye, and thanks for everything!

Just like Mr. Kalil—only he'd gotten out of their lives by threatening them. I shook my head. What was going on in me and with me?

I relaxed, attributing my feelings to too much wine. There was something else in the mix, however. Something brand-new crawling up and down my brain. And now I could identify it.

Fear.

SEVENTEEN

I awoke with a start. Someone was knocking officiously at my door. Tat tat tat. It was ten in the morning and I'd overslept.

"Come in," my voice squeaked, going up a register at its first use of the day.

"Good morning, sir. My apologies for waking you," Kingsley said. "Mr. Caeser requests that you join the family in the library."

"Something up?" I asked with a big fake smile.

"Mr. Caeser would have to tell you that, sir."

Suddenly I was conscious that I could hear far off, from outside, the hum of voices. Just barely. I took a quick shower, slipped into my clothes, and walked the mile (it seemed that way) to the library, where I found the family sitting there exactly as the night before. But there was something else in the air, a tension, a breathlessness. On Justin's face was a new bandage. They barely noticed my entrance, each off in his or her own world. Nobody was making contact. They may as well have been in separate parts of the house.

I realized that Eleanor was absent.

"Sit down, sir," Mr. Caeser said, sounding like a funeral director. "I'm afraid there's been some distressing news, terrible news. Shocking." He looked about.

Justin echoed, "Shocking." Mrs. Caeser stifled a moan. Mr. Caeser waited and I wondered, are we going to play Twenty Questions again? I shook my head sadly as if I knew what there was to be sad about.

"Dear Timothy is gone," Mr. Caeser said, and let it rest there.

I wasn't one bit surprised. I had the feeling that he was going to get out of there. He was miserable, terrified, and a lush. "Any idea where?" I asked.

"The ocean," Mrs. Caeser said, as if it had just come up in the tea leaves.

"He has taken his life," Mr. Caeser said, and breathed deeply, the sound full of sorrow and regret.

"Oh my God," I said.

Mrs. Caeser made the sign of the cross.

"His clothes were found on the beach, all of them. It appears that poor Timothy walked into the ocean," Mr. Caeser said, in what I found a tentative voice, as if he was trying his words on for size. "Even as we speak, sheriff's divers are out dredging, searching for a body. But that, that is a big ocean."

"They'll never find it," Justin said, and there was nothing tentative in his voice. He sounded as if he was stating a fact.

His father's bushy eyebrows shot up.

"I mean in that ocean, that angry and limitless ocean," Justin quickly added.

"He was no doubt drunk," Mrs. Caeser said in a rather uncharitable way for such a religious woman.

"It had grown steadily more noticeable," Mr. Caeser said. "But Eleanor never complained. Not once. The Caesers have learned to suffer in silence. Well, what was I to say? If she was satisfied . . ." He shrugged.

"How is Eleanor?" I said.

"As you can imagine," her mother said. "She loved Timothy very much. We all did. Timothy brought out that lovely quality in all who crossed his path." It sounded as if she was delivering the eulogy.

Justin said, "He was like a brother. The brother I never had." I wondered where I had heard that before. His mother patted his hand in commiseration.

Mr. Caeser nodded, dabbed at his eyes with a handkerchief, and said, "Like a son."

"I'm so sorry," I said. "Is there anything I can do?"

I had the feeling they had been waiting to hear me say those exact words. "Go to her," Mrs. Caeser said, her words almost falling on top of mine.

"Me?"

"She's fond of you," Justin said, and the way that he said *fond* didn't sound nice.

"She'll need your strength," Mrs. Caeser said, smiling warmly. "The rest of us are depleted."

"Where is she?" I said, standing.

"In her studio, her territory. Kingsley will take you," Mrs. Caeser said. I walked to the door, when Mr. Caeser called out, "Young man!"

I turned.

"Where is your ring?" he asked.

"My ring?"

"The ring I presented to you last evening."

"Oh, my ring! Last night—oh, I'm embarrassed to say

this," I said, thinking furiously, What in the hell was I going to say?

"Say it," Mr. Caeser said quietly. It was an order.

"Last night I put it beneath my pillow, like a talisman. A childish habit . . ."

None of them smiled at my little explanation.

"Wear it," Mr. Caeser said.

I tapped at the studio door, feeling both foolish and curious, like I was on a date, standing on somebody's front porch, waiting for a suspicious parent to open the door. What was *I* doing comforting her?

She told me to come in. It was a big room draped in shadows. Two paintings, covered with cloth, stood on easels and along a rear wall was a huge unfinished work. Or at least it looked that way to me. She sat with her back to me, on a high stool.

"It's me, Eleanor, and I'm so sorry."

A hand sneaked over her right shoulder and I went forward and took it. She turned and looked at me as if assessing me for the first time. She didn't say anything and I began inanely, "Life is so . . ."

"How big are you?"

"I beg your pardon?"

"Tall."

"Oh! Six feet. I'm six feet tall."

She wore a long forest green suede skirt that buttoned up the front and a short gold cable-knit sweater that had a hood. There were green suede boots, like riding boots, with straps and straps of green braid about the ankles. Her hair was down and framed her ivory face with those perfect features.

"How do you paint in here? It's so dark," I said, wanting to steer the conversation away from my physical endowments.

"Press that button," she said, pointing to a panel set into

the wall. I did and the ceiling silenty parted, giving her a huge skylight, now covered in light snow.

"Is that your current work?" I said, stepping closer to the large canvas.

"Yes."

It was pink and in it were tiny reddish and brown tendrils like follicles of hair. I wondered what it was about. I knew nothing about art. I then stepped over to the two covered paintings and moved to uncover them. "Don't," she said. I drew my hand back as if it had been slapped.

"I want you to see them when I want you to see them," she said, and I nodded as if I understood. She stepped off the stool and went to the big painting. Hands on hips, back to me, she said, "Well, what do you think?"

"I'm hardly an art critic," I said. I didn't know what I thought. To be honest, I thought nothing.

"You're hardly anything."

That stung. "Not so. I'm a human being. A male. A damn good lyricist. Let me think, what else . . ."

Those lush lips broke into a smile. "I struck a nerve. I had to. You sounded so goofy."

I smiled, too. My God, she was so gorgeous. And cruel. And spoiled. I said, "What is it?"

She looked at her work. "A vision of life, or at least the important thing in life. Does that sound vague? Don't let it."

"Life is pink?" I asked.

"Yes."

"And what are those little things extending out?"

"Realities. There's no perfection. Well, is there? Have you found any perfection?" she asked.

"Oh, I've come close a time or two. Mostly music. And you."

"Me?" She was amused and curious.

"You're near perfect."

"Near?"

"The parts of you that I can see certainly are."

"Just what other parts did you have in mind?" She licked her lips with the tiny tip of her tongue. I blinked.

"I mean the other parts of a person. You know. What do you think? What do you believe? What you really are," I said.

I had definitely disappointed her. "Oh. Those things."

Then we stood in silence. Finally, I said, "About Timothy . . ."

"Poor Timothy. I wonder why? We'll never know. He left no note. Still, you can't help wondering. Do you wonder why?"

"He must have been ill," I said blandly. She liked that and nodded. Then I said, "Or desperate." She didn't like that. Her face clouded over in anger, making her even more lovely. I believe she wanted to strike me or curse, but with some obvious effort took control of herself.

"Timothy had nothing to be desperate about," she said as if she were addressing a child. "He had inherited the earth. We had made him a part of this family. And he did have me. Not that bad a bargain, wouldn't you say?"

"No, of course not. But what was his part of it?" I said.

"His what? Just what are you gibbering about? Sometimes you sound like a Boy Scout!"

"I was a Boy Scout. An Eagle. What I meant was, what was Timothy's part, what was he expected to give or provide?"

"Himself. His wit. His intellect. His loins. I mean, what else would the Caesers need from anyone else?" Her eyebrows were lifted, her chin was up, the flow of her neck was glorious.

"Everyone needs," I said.

She smiled. "That's more like it. You don't sound like a juvenile at all. You're probably very clever. I believe I like you."

I nodded. "Your family has sent me here to comfort you. Am I doing it?"

"In your fashion," she said, and patted my hand.

"Good," I said, easing to the door.

"Someday I'll paint you," she said.

"Timothy predicted you might."

"Did he now?"

"The thing is, I may not want to be painted," I said.

"The thing is, you may not have any choice."

EIGHTEEN

In the morning, the biggest black Rolls I had ever seen sat parked at the front door. A uniformed chauffeur stood by stamping his feet against the cold. He saluted me and I saluted back. I believe it was the first time I had ever been saluted.

The family trooped out. They resembled one of those old photographs of the czar's family making the journey to the Winter Palace. The ladies were in full-length sable coats. Mrs. Caeser's was adorned with rhinestone buttons (I guess they were rhinestone). Justin's coat was cashmere and Mr. Caeser wore wool with a beaver collar. Both men wore wool touring caps and Mr. Caeser carried an ebony cane with a gold handle. It looked like a magician's wand in his hand.

Mr. Caeser spotted me and motioned me over. "It's a sad day," he intoned. "We are off to a coroner's jury in the village."

"Shouldn't I go along?" I asked.

The family smiled, sadly. "The village is not even aware

of your existence. Why should you get involved in this unpleasantness?"

Poor Timothy had gone from tragedy to unpleasantness rather quickly, I thought.

"Did you want to testify about anything in particular?" Justin said warmly, and I wanted to knock his cap off his head.

"What do you know?" Eleanor said.

"Nothing," I said quickly, before Mr. Caeser, whom I realized I feared, joined in my interrogation.

Kingsley and three other retainers came out of the house with the luggage (I guess it was luggage). All of it matched and there was a crest on everything. Except the small ice chest. That had no crest. I wondered what it could possibly contain.

Mrs. Caeser said, "Following the inquest the plane will take us to the funeral in Boston."

"I'll be back tomorrow," Eleanor said.

"Of course," I said.

"Miss me?"

"Eleanor, you're making the young man blush," Mrs. Caeser said.

"Quite the contrary," Mr. Caeser said. "He's pleased. And why shouldn't he be?" He smacked his gloved hands together as if he was killing a fly. Winter, now, was really upon us. Little puffs of cold air jetted from our mouths as we spoke.

"Our Eleanor's a dish," Justin said, and gave me a big friendly wink. What was going on here? I just smiled. I was doing an awful lot of that but felt no particular joy.

"Use the library, the music room. Kingsley will see to your needs," Mrs. Caeser graciously said.

"Stay out of trouble," Justin said. He wasn't winking anymore.

His father seemed to stare right through me. "He's no fool."

Justin said, "I don't know."

"He's no fool," Mr. Caeser repeated, looking me in the eyes.

Kingsley piled blankets about their legs and the big limo glided gracefully out the driveway and down the mountainside. It looked like a battleship.

I had the place to myself.

I started to walk on the path that would lead down to the beach and the ocean, but there was a second level leading from the path, which I knew would take me to the garden. This level was as wooded as any forest and snow clung to tree branches as though holding on for dear life. I avoided the gardens. Instead, I set out among the trees, the pine, spruce, and hemlock.

The biting wind gave me a brace and the frozen air smelled so clear and crisp that my uneasy feelings lifted and I treaded along for sheer enjoyment. Had the boy Justin ever camped among these trees? Had Kingsley set up his tent and roasted his marshmallows? In my mind's eye, that's what I saw: Kingsley bowing and gravely offering Master Justin a goodie on the end of a golden stick. My laughter rang out in the woods and I'd have bet that was a rare sound. Justin really bothered me, irritated me even as he picked at my conscience. I didn't like him anymore. It really bothered me because heaven knows he had bestowed every generosity on me. He was too enigmatic, or maybe it was me, perhaps I was too curious. Our differences created tensions and out of tensions, dislike. I had no idea how he felt about me.

There was a subtext to everything he said. Like a guy telling a gal, "I love you," and underneath meaning, "If you'll only let me get into your pants." I felt that in our case the subtext was a price tag, and that didn't bother me so much, because I'd learned to expect one long before I came to this island. What bothered me was I had no idea what the price was.

"Shucks," I said aloud. Maybe it was the gaudy splendor of this world into which I had been thrust that was affecting me; maybe it had nothing to do with Justin at all.

Whatever was going on was robbing me of joy in this unbelievable experience and more important, a feeling of comradeship with Justin.

It occurred to me that *Laffin' at the Palace* might have to be finished someplace else.

Should I tell Justin my feelings? Absolutely, if they were getting in the way of our work. But how could I accuse him of always holding back when that was precisely what I was doing? Saying nothing. Not telling was not me at all! Had the luxury bought me? Silenced me? Was I well on the way to corruption? At some conscious level, I must have thought so, because there had to be a reason why I found their gift ring—even now on my finger—so repulsive. So why was I feeling so much and doing nothing about it?

Now I was deep into the woods that circled all the mountain. My boots crunched on the frozen ground and the tip of my nose felt like an icicle.

I knew. Of course I knew. I was sublimating the truth because I was not quite ready to deal with it. The problem was, it wouldn't stay sublimated. I said aloud, "I'm afraid."

Fear, something horrible and impending, had worked itself into the marrow of my bones. The chill in me had nothing to do with the weather. Of whom? Of what? Why did I feel so threatened? This was no fairy tale; no dragon or ogre lurked about. Even the ghost had turned out to be an exotic, piteous young woman. Perhaps the most human of them all. I wondered whether I'd see her again? I would go to her but where, in this fifty-two-room palace? Nor could I ask. If I did, I had the feeling that I would be betraying some confidence, some tenuous gesture to reach out. It would be sinful to damage that. I would have to wait on Annabel Lee.

The wind had come up and I knew I'd have to be getting back, when suddenly, without warning, I found myself up against a ten-foot-high chain-link fence with barbed wire across its top.

NINETEEN

I walked about its perimeter until I came to a gate secured with a large padlock. Leading from the gate was a trail through the woods, which I was certain would take me by a more direct route back to the house.

Within the fence were two bright galvanized-steel buildings. The larger of the two was about the size of a four-car garage; the other building was about half its size. On the side of the big building, up near the roof, was mounted some kind of engine. I heard its electronic hum.

The fence was a shock. It was the only sign of security that I had seen on the island. With the treasures that the house contained, I expected to find a lot more but had not.

I couldn't imagine what this prisonlike compound was doing stuck in the middle of the woods. Maybe it was the wind or the isolation of the setting, or the grim simplicity within that fence, but I found myself feeling frightened and desolate. I knew that I had stumbled into something that I would have been better off never finding.

The buildings were so bright, the fence so high, I thought of a concentration camp. There was something evil about them.

I examined the Yale lock. On television, the good guy picks them open with a nail file. There was as much chance of pulling that off as there was of my commanding the snow to stop. I am not handy with tools and never in my entire life have I been able to fix anything. On the other hand, my mother was near to being a master mechanic and could on occasion fix the family car! I had not inherited this part of her genetic composition.

No, the only way that I would ever get within those fences was with a key, and where I might locate that item, I could not even guess. I certainly couldn't imagine the Caesers walking about with a bunch of keys on their belts. Nor had I ever seen Kingsley with a key. Maybe on a hook someplace, waiting for me.

Hey, I said to myself, hold on! What am I thinking? How did I make that mental leap from locked fence to Marion Anderson having to get inside the locked fence? Yet, that is precisely what I had done. It was natural. I had to get inside! Why?

I knew that whatever was there concerned me. How did I know this? I have no idea. I knew it, however, like some days you wake up and you know it's going to be a good day.

So where would keys be kept? In a drawer? That's where my mother kept them. A kitchen drawer? A drawer in that big desk in the library? No, the keys would have to be in someone's charge, and that someone had to be Kingsley. The keeper of the keys. A search of that house would take only a couple of years.

You've got to start someplace. I accepted that Kingsley would be in charge of the keys, so the keys had to be convenient to him.

The trees began to throw shadows, so I headed back to the house. Kingsley was hovering about the hall, a worried look on his face, and when he saw me I could see him fight down asking me where I'd been.

"This is some house," I said, wanting to draw him out. He said, "Yessir."

"Those Chinese pieces, how old are they?"

He paused for a moment, as if he was wondering whether he should answer my question. "They first reached Europe in Marco Polo's time, sir."

"I'm surprised there's no security on this island," I said. "There's a fortune in art treasures just lying about."

He smiled. "The Caesers don't require security, sir."

"Doesn't anyone ever cross the bridge without permission? This island seems so accessible."

"Not in my memory, sir."

"How long is that, Kingsley?"

"I am sixty-four, sir."

"No, I mean how long have you worked for the Caesers?"

"I am the third generation of my family to do so." He turned to go, obviously having used up a ten-year quota of answers. Still, I plowed on. "How about the other servants?"

"All from the village, where a bus picks them up in the morning and delivers them back in the evening."

"May I ask how many? Servants."

"There are forty or so, sir."

"This is some establishment!"

He motioned with his body that he wanted to depart. I said, "Kingsley, I believe I'll have sandwiches this evening in my room. With a couple of cold beers. That okay?"

"Whatever you wish, sir."

"What kind of beer do you have?"

"Samuel Adams, Rodenbach, La Belle Strasbourgeoise, Gamichlaus, Silver Dragon, Old Heurich, Ur-Bock Pale, and Claus Haler."

"Make it a good old Claus Haler. We went to school together."

He departed. I gave the lions a hello pat and went up

the stairs to my room. I had stripped down, showered, and put on pajamas and robe when I saw it. A pale blue envelope lay on my pillow. I opened it. At its top was the Caeser crest. The message was in black ink and resembled calligraphy.

"Please come and dine with me. Midnight. I am on the third floor. Take a left at the very top of the stairs, walk exactly forty paces. Come quietly." It was not signed.

I felt good! I didn't believe that Annabel Lee had had many people up for a midnight dinner. I felt that I had accomplished something good, and that, too, was one of my needs. I lay back on the bed, hands behind my head, and must have dozed off. Kingsley awakened me with a tray.

It was filled with a variety of sandwiches and a couple of ice-cold Claus Halers in a silver bucket. "Just what am I eating?" I asked Kingsley.

"Brown bread and crystallized ginger circles. Calla lily sandwiches. Cheese with olive flower. Toasted mushrooms."

"My favorites!" I said. "Just like Mom used to make."

There was a minor triumph written on his face—as if he had bested me in a tiny competition. "It's all like a dream," I said, and when he was at the door, his back to me, I added, "or a nightmare."

He stopped short. Turned. "I beg your pardon, sir?" He stood there, body language demanding an explanation. He was not an intimidating figure. I could have thrown him through the window with his tray of goodies. I stared back. He lowered his eyes first, gave what looked like a sad nod, and was gone.

I took the tray into the bathroom and one by one dumped those esoteric delicacies down the commode, all the time thinking of the horror on my father's face could he see me. He was the frugal one in our family, much given to the admonition "Waste not, want not" and reminders of "the children in Bangladesh."

I sat on the bed, made the acquaintance of Claus Haler, and waited for midnight and Annabel Lee.

TWENTY

I lay on my side and watched the snow. My life had changed so. The few days that I had been among the Caesers seemed like years. I had changed and not for the better. I had become wary, a quality that robbed me of an innocence that I cherished. And suspicious. I was taking a second and third look at everything, analyzing not only what people said but the looks on their faces. In other words, I had become paranoid. If I'd had a gun, I would have started carrying it on my person.

Justin also represented a personal loss. For more than a year, we had worked together in the remarkable kinship of creative effort. It had made us closer than brothers, susceptible to each other's physical condition as well as every psychological nuance. We really knew each other and we liked what we knew, despite the flaws that each possessed.

That was gone. It was as if a bridge that would always separate us had been built in a night, while we slept.

And Timothy. Timothy removing his clothes in that bitter wind and walking into the ocean. The freezing ocean. Why had he done it? He had been unhappy and he had been terrified, that I knew. But I never thought that his life had reached a point where he would end it. I simply had not possessed the analytic ability to gauge his despair.

I owed Timothy something. He had warned me and I was in his debt. Paying a debt to the dead is almost impossible. And meaningless.

I thought, too, of the bartender back in the village, what was his name, Johnny, Johnny Atooza! He had warned me, too. His warning was as fresh before my eyes as when it happened, because I could still smell his breath, feel the heat from his face pressed up against mine in that small bathroom.

Did I owe him a debt, too?

Of course I was in danger. I had no more doubt about that. So why didn't I gather up my handful of possessions, mostly my manuscript, and get off that island?

Choices. We make them.

I was titillated, intrigued by whatever it was that I had fallen into. If there was more to know, I wanted to know it. I wanted to know it all. And I was stubborn. This was one of those rare things on which both my parents agreed. I was a bulldog who wouldn't let go—no matter the consequences.

What did I want? What was the price I attached to the danger in which I felt certain I was enmeshed? To bring them down, the whole pompous, run-over-people bunch of them? Was that my aim? But why them? And why me the instrument of some kind of revenge I couldn't even fathom?

Questions! So damn many questions. And so few answers.

I dressed, turned off the lights, and peeped into the hall, so vast, empty, and dark. I went up the stairs to the third floor, counted forty paces, and saw that the door on my left had been left open a crack, wan light filtering out. I tapped softly and swung it open.

She wore a blue (always in blue) silk hostess gown and her hair was up. I stared at her. All lights in the apartment were muted. She said, "Please don't. Stare."

"You look like a swan," I said.

"A goose."

"No. A swan."

"A dying swan?"

"A lovely swan."

One of Grieg's piano concertos was coming from all around us; we were enveloped in loveliness. "Welcome to my world," she said.

Her world, a large apartment, was lined with books on every wall. The child who had sneaked into my room was not evident in the heavyweight material on her bookshelves. "I am honored to be here," I said, bowing. She brought out the formal in me.

"Look at me," she said, "look all you want. Here, I'll get close. Then please don't do it again."

I didn't, but turned away and walked about the spacious apartment. It, like her, was a surprise, as distant from the Caeser's lifestyle as I could have imagined.

The furnishings were white wicker. Her bed had a scalloped canopy covered in blue gingham ruffles. There was an old-fashioned—it looked like the fifties—vanity with a huge oval mirror and a white wicker stool. The floors were hardwood with little needlepoint rugs that slid when you walked on them. A curtain in blue check completely covered a big picture window, the rod heavy teakwood. The bookshelves were also white wicker and seemed too delicate to support the massive amount of heavy scientific and technical volumes—mostly from university presses—that they held.

On the vanity was an impressive collection of hair combs, some copper with jewels and some hand-carved ivory. I smiled.

"A person needs a hobby," she said. "Well?"

I didn't know what she wanted.

"My world. Your opinion."

"It's very lovely," I said, "like its occupant."

"Are you angry?" she asked.

"Why no, should I be?"

"Look at your hands, they're clenched. And your jaw is working like you're chewing gum. Are you always so up-tight?" she asked.

"I'm afraid it's a recent acquisition," I said. Would she pursue my words?

"Recent? Since . . ."

"Yes. Since I came here," I said.

"Sit down. Would you like some wine?"

"Would you happen to have a beer?"

She laughed. "I thought so! There's something beer about you. Will a Carling do?"

"My preference," I said.

It was great to be back to good old Carling. Anything simple, down-to-earth, nonexotic was suddenly sheer pleasure. Except Annabel Lee. She was exotic but pleasure, too. "Aren't you going to have anything?" I asked.

"Iced tea. I can't drink. It makes me break out in splotches. Would you believe white splotches?"

We laughed aloud.

"Tell me about you," I said, settling into a high-backed wicker chair. Legs crossed, I felt like a model in a high-fashion ad.

"I have had an unusual if not very eventful life. At a very early age, physicians determined that I suffered from a rare disorder that made sunlight unbearably painful. That was that as far as any kind of normal existence. My sentence was to be a hothouse flower."

"That painful?"

"Like needles, a million hot needles, sticking you all at once. I barely remember it but I do recall its horror." She shivered, then stood. "Would you excuse me? I'd better check on dinner."

She returned a few moments later with a fresh Carling. I said, "Please go on."

"Go on where?" she said. "That was the catch, don't you see? There was no place to go. So this apartment was designed and built for me, and when I was older, I decorated it according to my tastes. It's a lovely prison, don't you think?"

"Education?"

"What? Oh you mean my education. Tutors, the finest in their disciplines, paid huge sums to stay here for a semester, do their own work in luxury and teach me. I've even been tutored by Nobel laureates. When you're a Caeser, all things are possible."

"I believe that."

"I have a Ph.D. in anthropology. I study man, with whom I have no contact. It gives me a certain vantage point, a distance that's not all that bad in scholarly research."

"You're quite amazing," I said.

"Any other questions?" she asked, brushing my compliment aside. "For God's sake, let's get all that behind us."

"Just one. Your relationship with your family." This was for me the key question. Where would she stand if . . .

"I join them or don't join them as I choose. They are totally understanding and completely supportive. No one could ask for more. That support makes my life bearable, if not normal. The Caesers are one."

I tried a different tack. "I was thinking about Timothy."

"Dear Timothy," she said, and sounded sad. "He was a kind man and very learned. Did you know that Timothy had degrees from both Harvard and Oxford? With honors from both. We used to talk. He had read everything. We were, I think, close. At least in the beginning, and then . . . then . . ."

"Yes?"

"Timothy came down with that disease that is so easy to catch among us," she said.

"Disease?"

"I call it Caeseritis. Don't you think that's funny?"

"I'm sure it will be, but not quite yet."

"There, that anger is on your face again. Relax," she said.

"You were talking about Caeseritis."

"You sound like a prosecutor and I am not on the witness stand. It's a very unattractive quality."

"I apologize. Just curious, that's all," I said with a grin that perhaps I carried off.

"There, I prefer you that way. You're attractive again." She peered at me through those black holes, then burst out laughing. "You are a person who invites teasing. Did you know you may be just a tad pompous?" She reached out and lightly tweaked my nose. "You're so serious. Or maybe you aren't. Maybe you're just reacting to me. I do bring out such different feelings in people. Shock. Pity. Which?"

"You're not like the others," I said.

She stopped smiling. "Oh yes, I am. Do not let the pigment of my skin deceive you."

"About Timothy's disease," I said. "Caeseritis."

"As in owning the earth. Possessing everything. Everything. Wish, whim, fantasy, dream, available, suddenly all available, and if it isn't, it will be very quickly. Not everyone can handle that. I don't think Timothy could. He stopped doing anything but drinking. Out of that came guilt. And out of that, his death."

"You believe he killed himself?"

For an instant, the white mask of her face wrinkled up like a Kleenex crumpling. She said coldly, "I don't believe I know what you're talking about."

"Well, nobody really knows what happened to him. There were no witnesses."

"I think you'd better go." She stood.

"Why? Because I dared to differ or suggest some other vague explanation? What rules does that violate? You said the Caesers could possess everything, but that's not completely true!"

"Shh, you're shouting," she hissed.

"The Caesers do not own my mind, not now and not tomorrow. I reserve that to me and there is no price tag attached. I am a thinking creature and do not plan to stop being one until I die." I stood. "Forgive me for interjecting reality into this . . ."

"Cage," she said.

I collapsed back into the wicker. "I'm sorry."

She sat down. "Me, too. I'm not used to people, to conversation, to the opinion of others. The family agrees on everything. It's like we function with one mind. I must sound foolish. That's probably what I am. Do forgive me."

"Let's forgive each other," I said, extending a hand. She reached out and took it and I brought her hand to my lips and kissed it. And then there was embarrassed silence.

"I'll get dinner," she said, and went into the kitchen.

It was some dinner. We began with cream of artichoke soup with little homemade croissants. Then came vegetable pie with filo crust stuffed with chanterelles, morels, leek, tomato, barley, red onions, and goat cheese. And there were steamed clams in a light garlic sauce. We topped it off with fresh figs. All of it wonderful!

"Gee, what delightful and imaginative cooking," I said.

"You didn't miss a meat course?"

"No. Gracious no! Your family has spoiled me to . . ." I was about to say *death*, but somehow it seemed inappropriate. "Pieces," I finished my sentence.

"Oh, I'm glad you feel that way. I'm a vegetarian."

"Are you really?" I felt crazy, lighthearted. "I'm glad!"

"You're a strange one," she said. "You make *me* feel normal."

I stood. "Thank you for a lovely evening."

"I've never done this before. Had anyone in for a midnight supper, though I used to cook for my tutors all of the time. I believe I like it."

"May I kiss you good night?"

"I've never done that, either."

I drew her to me and kissed her cheek. Her eyes were closed as if she expected more, so I kissed her lightly on the lips. Those terrifying black eyes fluttered open. Was there amusement on her face? Impossible!

"I liked it," she said.

TWENTY-ONE

The next afternoon found me high up in the library going through the Caesers' astonishing collection of books, which would have been the envy of any other library, museum, or archive in the world. I heard the door open below, looked over the balcony as Justin looked up. "I thought you might be here."

I came down the narrow stairs and he extended a hand in greeting. I returned his grip in a less-than-enthusiastic manner and he blushed. "Let's talk," he said, motioning to side-by-side chairs across from the big desk. We sat and he cocked a leg over the arm, looked at his handsome hand-made riding boots and then at me. He was giving a lot of thought to something, probably me. I had not been too subtle.

"I don't like the way things are going between us. I don't like it at all."

I believe that's exactly what I wanted to hear. I stood

and said, "I can leave right now." I felt relieved. An out, and one offered by him.

"Sit down," he ordered, and then, "please."

I smiled and his eyebrows went up quizzically. "Joke?"

"No. I was just remembering the first time we met, or rather the first time I heard your music. I was enchanted. I'm not enchanted anymore."

"It seems like so long ago," he said, as if he was reaching way back for a memory.

"A year. A few weeks. Not too long."

"What's happened to us?" he asked, his hands making the gesture of brushing away cobwebs.

"We don't like each other anymore. That's all," I said.

"Yes. Things do seem to have gone awry. It was wrong to come here; I knew that but how could I say it? We haven't fared well. Perhaps it was inevitable. I don't know. I don't understand. But that's the way . . ."

"There's an unbearable tension here, Justin, an undercurrent, things unspoken, secrets. Bad secrets, I would say. I'm not certain that anything creative, as in free of constraints, can come out of this place, it's been locked into a certain position for so long. There's no room for flexibility. I'm sure it's no one's fault. It's just been that way for so long. . . . Maybe people don't belong on the top of a mountain or on an island."

"Yes," he said. "I thought it might turn out this way. I guess that's why, in my entire life, I never tried anything, not a single thing, like this, like what we're doing. I mean with someone else. Anyone else."

"In all fairness, it might have worked with a different type than me. Constraints go against my grain. I have the need to kick over the traces and gallop all over the damn place," I said.

"It's me. I don't know how to handle—that's a lousy choice of word, *handle*—what I mean to say is, I don't seem to know how to participate in a relationship, or even how to react to the needs of others. I mean the real needs, not food or drink. My life has made me perfunctory. I'm not even certain that I've anything beneath the surface. I may be all surface."

He stood and paced the room, running his long fingers over the gold-bound volumes. "It bothers me. What's happened between us bothers me greatly. More than you can ever imagine."

"I can imagine," I said coldly.

He paid my words no attention. "I discussed it with my family. Goddammit, don't sit there so blasé! It matters. You are not just someone. You are, or were, my friend and my colleague and I've never had either, and in all certainty I will never have either again. But forget me. The work. I really do believe we've got something. Not perfect but getting there. Not yet valid but right on it. Do you have any idea what that means? To be productive, for the first time in my life to be productive!"

"Calm down, Justin. I'm right here, there's no reason to shout. You sound like your father, and he frightens me. I can't hear you if I'm frightened. Okay. The work matters to me, too. Yeah, I do think we've got something, or had something. But it's evaporating; it's melting in my fist. The light's gone off. It's true. You know it is."

He nodded. "It's true. My family said we should start over."

"Just like that?"

"Unless you have the need to assess some penalty. If you do, I'll take that, too. In other words, I plead guilty."

"Justin, I don't want to hurt you. That would give me no pleasure at all. But I really do believe I should leave here."

"My father says he'll back our show."

I stared at him. The world stopped. I heard neither ocean nor wind.

"So what do you say, huh, buddy?" He stood and extended his hand.

One of those moments. A choice is presented and you make it.

I reached out and for a moment we shook hands, and then like lovers, we embraced.

And that's how the Caesers purchased me.

TWENTY-TWO

Mr. Caeser peered intensely at the wine cascading from the decanter into his glass and said, "Nineteen fifty-nine Bordeaux, the vintage of the century." He tasted it, stared out at us like the prelude to a pronouncement, and nodded. "It truly is." Kingsley visibly sighed with relief.

I disagreed. Silently. I was sitting next to the vintage of the century. Tonight she was Miss World. I made no pretense. I looked. Her skirt was of billowy net poofed out in layers that looked like they would blow away. It was black with little gold flecks and tiny gold beads sewn into it. Her top looked like a corset, strapless, completely fitted and made out of soft-as-butter metallic gold leather. About her neck was a shawl of the same material as her skirt. It was fringed and draped behind her.

"Forgive me," I whispered.

She laughed a throaty laugh. "I love it!"

Mr. Caeser, with the ears of this nation's most advanced radar unit, said, "Did I hear the word *love*?"

"You did father! And so did I," said Justin, lifting his glass in a toast to love.

"Marion"—that was the first time Eleanor had ever

called me by my name—"complimented me, albeit silently, then apologized. I told him not to. The truth is, I agreed."

"The truth is," said Mrs. Caeser, "Eleanor loves compliments."

"Vanity, thy name is Eleanor," Justin said.

"Beauty, thy name is Eleanor," Mr. Caeser joined in. "Well, Marion, do you agree? Come sir, no time for compliments though, time for speech, the sweet music of words."

"Marion agrees," I said. The vintage of the century was loosening my tongue. I kept myself in check only by thinking of smoke rising from my father's pipe behind *The Wall Street Journal*.

The food arrived and the chitchat came to a screeching halt. You could feel them suck in their collective breath with anticipation. They stared at the platter as though if they blinked it might vanish. Roast prime ribs had their full attention.

I did not look at it.

I busied myself with a lobster mousse, shrimp, and clams and calamari in a red sauce. There was simply no way to escape their pleasure as they cooed and made little biting and sucking sounds of satisfaction that transcended pleasure. They were off in some other dimension, reserved just for them, where their taste buds drove them quite mad. I believe I could have announced that I was having a heart attack and nobody would have looked up.

Kingsley smiled on benevolently, joining in their pleasure, though vicariously. Once my eyes caught his and I do not believe he even recognized me.

They ate like sharks in a feeding frenzy, tearing flesh from bone. It looked like stock footage from an old Tarzan movie where piranha turn a carcass into a skeleton in moments.

Then they went off into that other zone, lips greasy, hands wet with gravy and juice. They could have been at prayer. Their eyes were closed and they leaned forward as if their bodies had collapsed. Mr. Caeser came out of it—whatever *it* was—first, his eyes ponderously opening, the movement labored, like coming out of deep sleep. He wiped his greasy lips daintily and smiled at no one in particular. The world was good.

Now the others were coming out of it. Their eyes seemed to glow with pleasure and I felt a cold chill travel down my spine. It was that meat, that abominable meat. The platter had been cleaned except for a few tiny scraps that they eyed but of which they did not partake.

"Such a taste," Mr. Caeser said, and burped behind his big hand. Mrs. Caeser squeezed his hand and I noticed that her finger, beneath that huge diamond, was greasy. I shuddered and gulped down the vintage of the century.

I had Justin's attention. He smiled and said, "We love you, Marion. We truly do." He appeared warm and genuine and Eleanor casually took my hand and held it above the tabletop as if it was the most natural thing in the world to do. At least her hand was clean.

"Come, sir, don't be embarrassed," Mr. Caeser said. "We are people who express our affections. We do not hide our true feelings because we do not have to."

"Give the lad time," Mrs. Caeser said. "He's not used to us."

"Well, he will be," Eleanor said, and squeezed my hand. I was certain that all took notice.

Mr. Caeser stirred restlessly at the head of the table. He had gone some time without utterance. "If this great house crumbled to dust tonight because of a storm or a bomb, its foundation would remain intact. And bits of timber and marble and granite would remain. Anyone who chanced onto this island would be able to tell, what? That something, a structure, a grand structure of some kind had been here." He motioned to Kingsley, who had been so intent upon his lecture that he had stopped pouring. Kingsley blushed. His master's glass was quickly refilled. Mr. Caeser savored the first swallow and continued his lecture for the evening.

"Alas, not so with our late beloved . . . Timothy." Now they all stirred. I don't believe they had expected that subject. "He was here, he is gone. Poof! Like some street conjurer's trick. He leaves no stone, no mortar remains behind to remind anyone interested enough to wonder, that anyone, anyone named Timothy even occupied this earth." He paused and Mrs. Caeser shed appropriate tears. Justin and his sister sat expressionless.

"It is incumbent upon those of us who knew this man to not let that be the case. And we never shall. As long as we live, he lives! I am tomorrow giving the law school at State a new library to be called the Timothy Hedgely the Third Memorial." We applauded; he nodded with satisfaction. "And having said that, let us speak no more of dark and tragic things."

Eleanor said, "Timothy will always be inside us."

Justin began to make choking sounds—he was either dying or laughing—when his father looked his way and turned him off with a single glance.

"Sorry," Justin said, "the wine went down the wrong way."

Mr. Caeser was not quite through. "And now, ladies and gentlemen, I am in the mood for Mr. George Gershwin. Are you up to it, Justin? Of course you are. Well then, to the music room!"

TWENTY-THREE

Our happy, drunk little group, Mr. Caeser leading the way like head elephant in the circus parade, traipsed into the music room. Eleanor held my hand as if I were a kid brother or favorite nephew.

Justin sat at the piano and just started playing, though that really doesn't do justice to his immense talents. Justin Caeser was a piano virtuoso, good enough for any concert hall! I had never heard Gershwin played better and Eleanor whispered to me that Mr. Caeser had invested in Gershwin's early shows.

Now we were listening to "Rhapsody in Blue" and drinking cognac XXVSOP and there was no world except the world in that room. The Caesers really did have the wherewithal to make reality vanish, to create their own reality, and oh but it was easy to sit back and blissfully drown in it. They were capable and willing to offer up heaven. I put the price of admission out of my mind and attributed it to Gershwin and cognac XXVSOP.

I smiled drunkenly and Eleanor kissed my cheek, a bit of her mouth accidently getting a bit of my mouth. Justin smiled approvingly at us. They had this talent of making you feel as if you were basking in a sun created just for you. At that moment, I loved the Caesers. Do I sound mad? Of course, I was mad.

The wine, the cognac, the sensual beat of Gershwin, the harpsichord casually in the corner (owned by Handel and played by Haydn), beautiful Eleanor holding on to me, well, can you blame me? And good old voluble Falstaff, Dad, Saint Nicholas, Mr. Caeser, just poised for us to give the word! The show is ready! The show is ready! And then, bingo, the money: Here, the money, is this enough? Need more? Here, take some more!

Out of town, then Broadway and it's opening night. Dad Caeser has booked Sardi's, the whole damn place, upstairs and downstairs, caviar and Mouton Rothschild for the five hundred guests (isn't that Mike Nichols and Diane Sawyer?) and what did the *Times* say? Phone rings. Silence. Our press agent answers. Listens. Grunts mysteriously. The rat. Turns to us, face blank, can't hold it in, screams above the rising din (because other people have picked up on what *he knows*), "We've got a hit!" Tears are streaming down my face. I can't wait to break through the adoring crowd to embrace my mother, lovely with the orchid corsage I gave her.

"Let's go fuck."

I was blinking.

"Are you drunk? Oh shit. You are."

"Huh?" I asked. "What did you say?" Reality was returning and it was so painful and shocking.

Eleanor shook her head. She was quite disgusted. Justin's smile had turned into a grin. He shook his head ruefully. She shrugged. She was adorable when she shrugged. Justin laughed. She laughed. Good sports. We were all good sports.

I have no idea how I got to my room or who undressed me and put me in pajamas. I suspect Kingsley, as I could not envision the family doing anything that mundane. I'm not certain they undress themselves.

I awakened, peered at my watch, and was shocked that only an hour had gone by. I turned over and remembered the evening, all of it. And remembering, became highly aroused. Her words, her invitation—I had heard it— would have gotten a response from a pine tree.

Why should the evening be over? I pondered this for all of half a second as I slipped into robe and slippers. I wanted her. I wanted her so much, I had difficulty making it through the door and then padding down the hall. I was humming "Bess, you is my woman now," with great emphasis on *now*.

"There is a time to live and a time to die and a time to" . . . now was that time. Visions of Eleanor naked, on her back, legs spread, waiting for me. I was at her door and turned the handle.

In the darkness, shadows, but not so dark that I could not decipher them. She was on her back, legs spread, Justin atop her, pounding madly away.

TWENTY-FOUR

I didn't go back to sleep. I had experienced my first case of instant sobriety. I just lay there replaying the image over and over like a movie projector that wouldn't stop.

I am a young man. Of my times. Very much with it. Nothing is supposed to really affect me. This did. There was something horrifying about brother and sister coupling like animals. Nothing in my experience had prepared me for it and I felt defenseless and debased. There was nothing erotic about it. I felt dirty, as if I had been injected into their act.

I am no prude. I've read Henry Miller and D. H. Lawrence and I've seen more than one porno flick. I went to some movies in Times Square when my mother thought I was at music stores. And I have had sex—not a lot, but some. Actually two times. Two different women and neither were prostitutes and one of the two was the aggressor. But this was something else!

This was downright dirty. Filthy. Perverse. And why did I feel that I was involved? The Caesers were hogs, rich hogs. And suddenly, just like that, I knew me! Call me Faust. Marion Anderson had sold his soul.

I felt empty, as if my insides had slipped out and left a bottomless cavern—a cold place. I sat hunched on my bed and wept as I have never wept before. I wept for me, or, more specifically, for my loss. I had crossed a line of demarcation and would, as long as I lived, never be the same again. I mourned my innocence and what I had given up.

In my misery, I arrived at a truth: Men do require rules. The Caesers had none, certainly not society's. They were wrong, dead wrong. Men need some kind of agenda to follow. There's got to be a North Star someplace to point the way.

I wanted to stop bawling. I tried. Suppose we were all Caesers? I attempted to envision a world that way, but it was too much for me. It took a Bosch or a Picasso to possess that kind of vision; my mind could not or would not make the leap.

The shower washed my tears away, but that's all that went down the drain. I stood there letting the hot water pound me for at least an hour in the time immemorial ritual of self-cleansing, cleaning of the flesh and what the flesh had been witness to. I got rid of the dirt outside but found no comfort inside. Oh God, but I could still see them and I shuddered at the thought of having to see them face to face. What would I say? Hello, you incestuous monsters. Good morning, you evil bastards!

I dressed and went down through the silent tomb of the house for coffee. Kingsley, now as warm to me as was the rest of the family, was distressed that coffee was all that I wanted. I told Kingsley that I was going to take a walk in the garden. "Dress warmly, sir, it's hovering at seven degrees."

I put on my bad-weather gear, courtesy of the Caesers, and went out to be greeted by a slate gray sky, ominous, leaden, dull, and promising nothing. Or maybe all that was in me. I felt nothing.

I was not alone. Mrs. Caeser was talking in fluent German to a scarecrow of a man. She wore a gorgeous heavy black wool coat. Her hands were in black kid gloves with matching low-heeled boots.

She introduced me to the man, a Herr Gustav Schiller, "our head horticulturist." We shook hands and with her permission he drifted off. "He was," she explained, "Hitler's chief gardener at Berchtesgaden. Though he finds speaking of those days quite painful."

"You can hardly blame him," I said.

She said, "Who knows, who knows?"

Who knows what? I thought. What did she have doubts about? Hitler?

"Six million Jews know," I said.

"Jews," she said, and I dropped the subject. She insisted on taking me on a tour of the garden. "The fountain is seventeenth century, from Bassano di Sutri, near Rome. The hedges are hemlock. The gardens will be beautiful in the spring and the summer. You'll love them. There, as far as you can see, forty thousand tulips, roses, and iris."

I followed her to a small pink marble bench full of intricate carvings. "This is the first time we've really gotten to talk," she said, "and I must admit to being curious about you."

"I'm afraid you're in for a letdown."

She smiled. "You're a very attractive young man," she said, her knee touching mine, "so young, yet your eyes are so grave."

I thought, If this lady gropes me, I'm going to run

screaming through the tulips. "My daughter is taken with you; she can't thank Justin enough for bringing you here."

Oh yes she can, I thought, and my face must have betrayed something. "What is wrong?" she asked.

"No! It's just that . . . well, I've never known anyone like the Caesers. It's well . . . confusing."

She laughed with delight. "There are no people like the Caesers," she said, patting my thigh in a friendly gesture. "But what specifically confuses you? The surroundings? In time, they'll become just a background, a setting and nothing more. Still, I can see that they must be overwhelming. They would affect anybody. Give it time."

"Actually, not the surroundings, astonishing though they are. I had no idea that anyplace like this really existed except in *Citizen Kane*. No, it's attitudes—oh, I don't know exactly how to express it. . . ."

She mussed my hair back. "Come, come, speak to me as you would your own mother or even a girl friend. Do you have one?"

"A mother? Of course. Oh, you mean a girl friend? No."

"Good. You will. Soon."

"Are you a mind reader or a seer, Mrs. Caeser?" I asked.

"I am both. I am reading your mind at this very moment and do believe me, dear Marion, I know your future."

"I'm not sure I want to know my future, but please go on, tell me what's on my mind!" I said all of this with a smile equal to her own. We were having a smile-out.

"Very well." She sighed. "You're wondering about Timothy. Well?"

It was astonishing! I stammered, "Yes."

"Specifically, you wonder about our attitude toward his death. You find it callous. Cold. Indifferent. You wonder just what kind of people we are. Well? Go on, don't be embarrassed, though I must admit I find you most attractive when you're blushing or stammering."

"You must find me attractive all of the time."

"You're a bright one; I like that. Timothy. Poor Timothy. We all called him that and in time it came to be his name. Why? Because he committed, what is for the Caesers, perhaps the only sin. Timothy squandered opportunity, opportunity that he fell heir to without any effort on his part. He came to us as an employee, an attorney with a genius in trusts. He and his firm were handsomely paid; the Caesers are among the most generous people on earth. My daughter found him attractive, a fancy I did not share. Ugh. You I find most attractive. At any rate, Eleanor and he became lovers under my roof. He had gained paradise. You agree?"

She was squeezing my thigh, above my knee, kneeding it as if it were dough. I nodded.

"Say it," she demanded. Her hand moved higher.

"Yes!" I shouted, "Eleanor is magnificent."

She patted me. Good boy. "So poor Timothy had it all, suddenly he had it all. And what did he do with it? You saw him. He became a lush. Timothy became poor Timothy. Perhaps he always had been. And despite that, the Caesers did not abandon him. If anything, my daughter gave him more love. I suspect that he, even in his stupor, was beginning to realize that even a golden egg can make a very messy omelet. And when he faced up to the truth . . . he took his life. A single noble act. He died better than he lived."

I should have kept my mouth shut. What did my words matter? I said, "I don't know."

Her dark visage grew darker, blood rushing to her face as if night had suddenly fallen on us. Her black eyes became pinpoints of blazing energy, directed at me. "What exactly do you not know?"

"How Timothy died."

She jumped to her feet, her hands clenched. I believe she wanted to strike me or scratch out my eyes. I sat there, face expressionless, heart pounding, looking up at her. She looked down at me, face so tight that it looked brittle enough to crumble. She sighed a great sigh and sat back down. Her fists unclenched and her eyes went from black to smoky, as if a film had drifted in over them. She smiled at me benevolently. I was an innocent child to be forgiven.

Softly, so softly I could barely hear her through the wind that was cutting at us like a rapier, she said, "How do you think poor Timothy died?"

"I don't know. I know that he was terrified, more terrified than I have ever seen. A fool could see it. And . . ." I hesitated, not knowing whether I should go on. "We spoke."

She bolted upright, her back as straight as a ramrod. "You spoke? What did he say?"

"He promised to meet me later, to tell me . . ."

"Tell you! Tell you? Tell you what? What did poor Timothy want to tell poor Marion?"

You evil bitch, I thought. "I don't know. He never showed. He vanished."

She simply could not keep the triumph from her voice. "Then really, you don't know anything."

"I guess I don't," I admitted.

"You have made me very angry, young man. Someplace in all of those 'I don't know's there is a hint of slander. Against the Caesers. We can't have that. We won't have it."

"I'm sorry," I said, but there was no apology in my voice.

She smiled, not a pretty smile. "I am a seer and I do know your fate."

"I believe I know yours, too," I said.

"Well, we'll certainly see, won't we?" she said, and whirled about and vanished, a dark figure in a frozen landscape.

TWENTY-FIVE

"God, that's so eloquent," I said. The melody he had composed to the almost childishly simple lyrics of a love ballad that I had written drifted like sun motes from the Steinway. "Exquisite," I said.

"No less than your words. The words unlocked the music. Sing it," he said, and I did in my whiskey tenor, a kind of lyric sandpaper. He was also a great accompanist.

"Justin, your talent is almost shameful. It's not right for a man to have so much."

He smiled with appreciation. "It is going well, isn't it?"

"I think we've got something, not wishful thinking, either. I really do," I said.

"I think so. In fact, I'm prepared to go with the first act as is. How does that strike you?"

"Oh heck yes. It's ready," I said.

"What do you say we perform it for the family?"

"That frightens me."

"Everything frightens you," he said. "You are a hysteric and a coward. But I love you. No doubt, for your weaknesses!"

"Sticks and stones." I laughed. "Justin, I think there's something I should tell you."

He struck a great dark chord. "Here we go again."

"I know and I'm sorry, but it's your mother," I said.

"My mother?"

"We had words in the garden. She was angry. I mean *angry*."

"Oh? About what?"

"Timothy," I said.

He studied the keys but made no move to play. "Leave poor Timothy be."

"Timothy won't let me be."

"Another ghost? That would be your second, wouldn't it?" he said.

"No, I haven't seen Timothy and I can explain the ghost," I blurted, and could have strangled myself for the stupidity.

"Explain."

"Explain?"

"The ghost. You said you could. Do it."

"I was drunk as a sailor on shore leave. I might as well have seen a flying saucer, been abducted to Pluto," I said.

He relaxed. "What a character you are. It's your charm."

"I never saw Timothy. It's what I think."

"Goddammit, what do you think?"

"I'm not sure Timothy killed himself," I said.

"Evidence?" He spat the word out.

"None. In fact, most things point to his doing just that, walking into the ocean. He was a piteous drunk, a subject I know something about," I said, trying to lighten the atmosphere, which was beginning to resemble a courtroom.

"Yes, you do, you beerhead. You Carlingaholic."

"He was frightened, Justin, as frightened as I've ever seen a person. He was going to talk to me about it."

"He was frightened, I can believe that. Alcoholics become extremely paranoid in the later stages of the disease, and Timothy was no beginner. Perhaps Timothy began seeing the proverbial pink elephants."

"But why would he want to see me? I'm hardly a psychiatrist or an alcohol counselor."

"No, I would not call you Sigmund Freud, but perhaps there is an explanation. Hear me out. Say Timothy wanted, needed to talk with someone, someone outside my family, someone with whom his conversation would place him in no jeopardy. That would be you. There's no one else. Haven't you ever just needed to talk with someone, especially when things were not going well and, believe me, they were not going well for Timothy. He was consuming more than a fifth of vodka a day that we knew of."

"Poor bastard." Why were we always attaching that adjective to Timothy's name?

"All right. What else? Let's get it all out so we can get on with our work," said Justin.

"Nothing, nothing else. What you say makes sense." I lied because the beginning of a plan was forming. It had begun when Mrs. Caeser said she knew my destiny.

He beamed, buying the package. Now it was time to reel the fish in. "Justin?"

He was back to creating music and didn't even look up. "Uh huh?"

"Would it be okay if I skip dinner this evening? I'd kind of like to get away, you know, think about what a fool I've been. Maybe I'll go into the village, have a beer, clear my head."

He didn't answer. It was as if he didn't hear me. He was into our score. "The truth is . . ." I began.

That got his attention. He looked up at me. "The truth?"

"I feel badly about my words with your mother. She's been so gracious to me. I want to buy her a gift. I don't know any other way to apologize. It's something I've got to do."

He loved it. "Sure. Get my car keys from Kingsley. I like the gesture. She'll appreciate it on one condition. Don't spend more than five bucks. That'll make your gift unique. The Caesers like unique things. Now come on, let's hit it."

We labored intensely for another couple of hours. I was

exhilarated, glad to be getting on with what I knew I had to do, and glad to be getting away from them for a little while.

It was all too close, that island, house, and, of course, them. They left you absolutely no breathing room and, oh, but I needed that.

I went upstairs to get my heavy jacket and gloves because outside the temperature was hovering at five degrees.

Kingsley was lurking in the hall like a ghoul in a Hollywood cheapie. I told him I'd need the car keys and he replied that Mr. Justin had informed him. And we stood there.

"The key, Kingsley, the key," I said, trying to sound like a plantation overseer.

He turned and I followed him. He stopped and said, "I'll bring it, sir; there's no need for you . . ."

"Kingsley, let's not make a big deal out of this. Just get the key," I ordered.

He turned and I followed him into the butler's pantry. There was a large cabinet on the wall, which he swung open, and there they were, dozens of keys, each neatly labeled. He quickly handed me Justin's car keys and slammed the cabinet shut before I could get a good look. "There's another set in the garage, sir. I'll have the car brought around."

"Thank you, Kingsley," I said, as if he'd just bestowed on me the Victoria Cross. I believe Kingsley looked me in the eyes for the first time since I'd met him and the look shocked me. It was filled with pure hatred, focused hatred, no attempt to hide it.

"Be careful, sir," he said so softly that I wasn't certain that I'd heard him as the front door shut behind me and the winter slapped my cheeks.

I shuddered at his look and at the cold and got into the car. Naturally, the heater had already been turned on and I was quite comfortable as I flipped on a Bangor station. It was so strange to hear the outside world, different voices, I could have been some astronaut, in my high-tech cocoon, coming in for a landing on some distant planet.

Cautiously, I made my way down the mountain and rumbled over the snow-covered bridge, feeling relief when the car's tires reached the other side and I was off that island. Those dim lights at either end of the bridge shimmered before and behind me as I entered the village's main street.

Grace possessed a very modern grocery store, a service station (closed for the evening), a small medical clinic that looked ancient, a pharmacy, and Ye Last Chance Tavern.

I pulled up in front of the pharmacy and walked through a narrow path that had been halfheartedly cleared through the snow.

A tinkling bell on the door announced my entrance and a big ugly woman, hair in an untidy bun, and wearing a dirty white smock, approached from a room behind the counter. I recognized her as the woman I'd seen drinking in Ye Last Chance Tavern that first night.

She was a shock to behold in fluorescent light from overhead. Her face was weather-beaten and there was the beginning of a mustache and broken capillaries in her cheeks that she had modestly attempted to cover over with rouge.

"May I help you?" she asked in a baritone voice. Between her big raw hands was a man's handkerchief that had been rolled up into a ball.

Only her eyes were alive and even youthful. They were a pretty brown, like the eyes of a fawn. They did not go with the rest of her. I saw recognition in her look; then it faded, as though she couldn't quite make the connection of where she'd seen me before.

"Good evening," I said. "I'm looking for a modest gift. For a woman. Someone who has everything."

"No one's got everything," she said, a challenge in her voice. Her words slurred. She'd already had a few. "In what price range?"

"That I know exactly. Five bucks."

She was unconsciously tying a knot in the handkerchief. She saw me staring and blushed, her fingers now untying it. "You look at people," she said. "Who are you?"

"I'm sorry. It's just good to see a stranger."

She smiled. Her teeth were stained. "Where you been? Jail?"

"On the island."

All expression on her face vanished. I could have been looking at cheap marble, and she shoved the handkerchief in a torn pocket of her smock. She cleared her throat nervously as though working through some cobwebs and smiled grimly. "I've some nice boxes of choc . . . choc . . ." She couldn't quite get the word out. "And handkerchiefs. Quite nice ones. We've a special on them. I overbought."

"Sure. Choose a nice lady's handkerchief for me, please. Do you gift wrap?"

"Oh yessir," she said, now sounding like a clerk trying to get on with the sale. I sensed much pain in this woman.

I followed her to the register and while she rang up the sale and wrapped the handkerchief in some pale blue paper, I said, "About me. I'm a guest on the island. I'm not one of them. A guest of Justin's . . . we're working on a project together."

I suddenly stopped. What was I doing gasping out explanations like a schoolboy who'd been caught? I shook my head. I didn't understand me. I handed her the money and she handed me the small package. We were suddenly formal, like signers of a treaty.

"Say, and please don't take this the wrong way, could I interest you in a drink over at the tavern? I really would enjoy talking with someone."

"Don't they talk?" she asked, face innocent.

"Someone different," I said.

"I don't drink," she said, and turned her back to me.

Lush, I thought angrily. I said, "I'd like to buy a pocket flashlight." She turned back to me, her bushy eyebrows up. "To find the bathroom at night," I said, disliking this woman intensely for somehow forcing me to offer explanations that were really none of her business. Her eyebrows came down; the deer eyes seemed to be taking another, more serious look at me. I stared back, paid her, and slipped the flashlight in my jacket pocket.

"If you change your mind, I'll be across the street," I said.

"You like our tavern, huh?"

"Actually, I don't know. I was just there that one time. That's where I saw you," I said.

She nodded. "Yeah. Sure. I thought I'd seen you before but I couldn't place it. You were with Mr. Justin."

"That's me," I said. "Actually, I want to talk with Johnny Atooza the bartender. He tried to do me a favor that night. Or at least I think he did."

"Johnny Atooza'll be kind of difficult to come by," she said.

My heart stopped. "He's not . . ."

"Dead? Johnny dead? Now why would you think a dismal thing like that? No, I don't think he's dead. Gone. He's just gone."

"Where? When?"

"Slow down, mister. This is a pharmacy, not a quiz show."

"Look lady, Miss . . ."

"Kole with a *K*. Polly, and that's with a *P*, Kole."

"I'm Marion with an *o*, Marion Anderson."

I extended a hand, which she looked at curiously. A furious thought process was under way in her head, a decision being reached. "We can shake hands after we know each other," she said, "and if we still want to."

"Good night, lady," I said, heading for the door.

"I could have sworn you offered me a drink," she said.

I stopped, turned to her, and said, "I could have sworn I got turned down."

"Bible says not to swear. Or maybe it was my preacher. Somebody said it." She began putting on a man's shapeless coat; it looked like army issue. She tied a gray scarf around her head and turned off the lights, plunging the pharmacy into darkness. I waited while she locked up and put a sign in the door. "IN EMERGENCY, I AM AT YE LAST CHANCE TAVERN."

We crossed the street and went inside. It was occupied by a few quiet people into their own thoughts and tap beer. She had a certain table off in a corner, a kind of place of honor, a drinker's table, a serious drinker's assigned spot.

A young guy in aviator glasses and bangs combed artfully over his forehead to cover a skull that would soon be bald brought her a bottle of rye, a bucket of ice, and a couple of glasses. I ordered a beer. She took off her coat and hung it over the back of her chair, where it lay partially on the floor.

She wasn't interested in anything but the rye. You could tell that was what her life was built around.

She toasted me. "Here's to a long life." Then she laughed in such an ugly way that the bar's other occupants looked up at us from their solitude.

She killed the rye as though it were an old, familiar enemy and went back to the bottle for seconds. I wondered how long she could go on before she passed out. "What happened to Johnny Atooza?" I asked.

"Reedle!" she shouted, and the man in the aviator glasses came over. I was certain that she was Ye Last Chance Tavern's best customer. She had begun to run her hand across her eyes. She must have done a lot of that; the skin was rough and red. "Man wants to know about Johnny."

Reedle laughed with delight. He enjoyed telling this story. "I've been tryin' to buy this place from Johnny forever. Me and him go way back. One night, just like that"—he snapped his fingers—"Johnny calls, and would you believe he's ready to sell? I knew he wasn't drunk because Johnny didn't drink. One stipulation, it's got to be right then. And that's how we cut the deal, right then, just like that. Johnny was leaving Grace forever. We met here. I gave him a postdated check—we knew each other pretty good, like I say, we go way back—and Johnny got his jacket and hauled. Now ain't that the damnedest?"

"Ain't that the damnedest," Polly parroted, and when he'd drifted away, asked, "That story mean anything to you?"

"I can't imagine that it would."

"Happened the night you and Mr. Justin were in here. Now you tell me," she said.

I was confused. "Tell you what?"

"Listen, you pip-squeak, don't bullshit a bullshitter! What happened that night?"

How much did I want this drunk to know?

"I am an alcoholic," she said, "but I am a lady of certain dignity."

I believed her. Why? Maybe because I had to, had to believe somebody. I whispered, "Johnny warned me about the island."

She nodded. "Johnny Atooza was that kind of man."

"He told me not to go there."

"He tried to do you a favor," she said, and drank to it.

"I didn't understand. What did I know?"

"You understand now, don't you? Well? Don't just sit there, goddammit, answer me."

"Shh, you're shouting," I said.

"I asked you a question: Do you understand now?"

"Yes. I understand."

"What else happened?"

"Happened?" I asked stupidly.

"Happened!" she shouted, demanding an answer with her glass, as if it were a policeman's baton.

I sipped my beer to slow down; I didn't like the feeling that I was part of an unruly mob. "I was in the john and Atooza came in and suddenly he was warning me. Then Justin was there with us; it was ridiculous really, three of us shoved into that little room. It got more ridiculous because suddenly Johnny and I were lying and trying to explain ourselves to Justin, like he was God and our lives depended on it."

"That's the Caesers all right; they make you feel that way without even trying. Did he say anything to Johnny?" she asked.

"Well, not exactly."

"Be exact," she ordered. She was a strong dame, drunk or sober.

"Justin said he'd be seeing him."

She nodded. The bottle was dead; she placed it on its side. "Well, there you are. Johnny got while the getting was good! Johnny Atooza was no fool. He was also a good man."

"Sure."

"You punk, don't 'sure' me! The man tried to warn you. Appreciate that. He didn't have to, you know. You were a complete stranger. That little good deed forced him to change his life. Reedle! Bring me a bottle so's I can toast good deeds that wreck good men." She looked sad, like she wanted to cry.

"What's the matter with you, lady?" I asked when Reedle had left the new bottle. I noticed he didn't touch the one that was on its side, as if he didn't want to disturb its sleep.

First she had a long slow drink. Everything else came way after that. "I am a lady in mourning," she said soberly. Now her eyes were wet. Memory was killing her.

"Tell me, Polly," I said.

"You are one inquisitive young fellow. Sure. I'll tell you. Then you know what? Do you know what?"

I just sat there.

"Then I want you to get in that pimp car and get the hell out of here, out of Grace, out of these parts. I want you to go away and forget it. What's the use, huh? My slogan, what's the use."

"Tell me."

"My brother L.C., Lafcadio Charles Kole." The slur was now more pronounced and the sadness was thick enough to touch. "A happy-go-lucky, whistling-like-a-bird fellow. Interested in orni . . . orni . . . you know . . ."

"Ornithology."

"Birds. A whistling man studying birds. Put on hold for a moment, well that's what he said, when Vietnam came along. Did it come along or did L.C. go get it?" Her hand was cocked like a trigger and she was pointing it at me.

Another Vietnam story, I thought.

"L.C. the joyous went. To Vietnam. The Marines were looking for a few good men. L.C. was a good man. Well, the first day there, the first hour of the first day, a sniper stopped the whistling. Split L.C.'s face in half, but both halves were L.C." She took a swallow to that. "They put L.C.'s face back together, sort of—they are not magicians, just physicians. But naturally there was a scar, right down the middle of his face. No complaints. L.C. was goddamn lucky to be alive. Or at any rate, I thought so. I don't know what he thought, because L.C. came home different than he went away. He came back different in more than his face."

I didn't want to hear any more. She knew it and smiled. God could not have stopped her. "L.C. would get on something and become downright fanatic. Ever had to deal with a fanatic? First the Bible, the Good Book, Old and New Testaments. He read it day and night, through and through, sometimes aloud. Then he set out to memorize it. He lived with me, L.C. did, and one day I asked how his studying was going. Know what L.C. said? 'What studying?' He wasn't joking, kid."

She rubbed her forehead as if she had a headache. "Let

me think, let me drink. What was next? Oh yeah, piano. He taught himself to play and, dammit, L.C. played good. Real good. Reedle!"

"Yeah, Polly?"

"How good was my brother on the piano?"

"Professional," aviator glasses said. "He could have played with any dance band."

"See," she said, and toasted her brother at the piano in her mind. "Then he stopped. Forgot everything he learned, bang, like that. Hell, he couldn't play chopsticks. He looked at the piano I'd bought him and he couldn't even remember what it was for. It's still sitting there in my parlor. I keep the curtain closed but the piano is there. Would you like to buy a piano?"

I shook my head and I thought, That's the thing about asking questions of people you don't really know. Some-times the answers kill you.

"And then L.C. got on pirates. P-i-r-a-t-e-s. You know, yo ho ho and a bottle of rum! Old maps and old books and then I realized that it wasn't pirates my poor brother had gotten himself interested in, but pirates' treasure. Cap-tain Kidd. Naturally. My brother and his faded maps and his faded life, all past tense, even his future was past tense . . . and oh but I am drunk, thank God for little wet favors. Well, he believed that Captain Kidd had buried his treasure someplace around here. Want to guess? Go on, win yourself a Kewpie doll, take a guess."

"Caeser Island."

"Naturally. Based on legend, and it is legend, just leg-end, but dammit the legend does exist, Captain Kidd's treasure was right here, waiting like golden cherries for the picking. Was I the dutiful sis? Better believe it. I loved L.C. even the way he was, scar, face that didn't match up, bullshit pirates, everything! I bought him a metal detector. Hell, I'd of bought him a Geiger counter. I begged him to leave those people and their island alone. But it was like making an appeal to a grin, because that's what he did: grin. Ever argue with a grin? You lose every time.

"I'm not sure he persisted; maybe the grin was listening, maybe not; maybe it just didn't know how to reply. You can lose a reply you know, just like you can lose a brother. He'd set out in his boat and go search for Captain Kidd's treasure, harmless enough, I guess. And then, one day L.C. didn't come back. L.C. just by God didn't come back.

"The sheriff looked, the coast guard looked, the Caesers offered a ten-thousand-dollar reward for anybody having information to L.C.'s whereabouts. Everybody in Grace looked, looked on the beach and in the water and in the woods, wherever a grin might slip off to.

"But he was gone. Poor fellow, one way or another, war or peace, my brother was not to come home.

"And I am alone," she said, and her head hit her chest and she began to snore and I went to help her, but someone said, "Leave her be. We will take care of Polly Kole."

TWENTY-SIX

I was half-asleep when my eyes flew open, aware that someone else was in the room. I cursed myself for not having put my newly acquired pocket flashlight beneath my pillow. Instead, it was in the pocket of my pants, which were hung over the back of a chair. I lay there like a sacrificial lamb awaiting I knew not what. My adrenaline was not rushing to the right places and fear had rendered me immobile.

It just wasn't like in the movies or I would have leaped

from the bed into a martial-arts defensive posture, ready to send a flying kick to the head of whoever had entered my space without my permission.

I was more like a senior citizen in a wheelchair.

Nor did any prayers come to mind. I believe I said, "God," but that was the extent of my call for divine intervention. My systems had shut down and I felt the stirrings of anger at my ineptitude (why hadn't I studied kung fu?) and my cowardice. I was afraid. My fear had come into fruition in bits and pieces, like a jigsaw puzzle. Now, suddenly, there it was.

I said to myself over and over, "It's not like in books, it's not like in books," and though this gave me absolutely no comfort, it became a kind of mantra.

Nor did I speak out: Who goes there? It either never occurred to me or my vocal cords had ceased functioning. I might as well have been trussed up, waiting for my destiny.

"Shhh," the other figure hissed, then hands pushed me back against the pillow, gentle but strong hands. A woman's hands with long fingers and a tiny wrist that I could encircle with my hands—and my hands were not what you would call woodchopper's hands.

The woman's hands were unbuttoning my pajama jacket and then slipping it off my shoulders. And then lips were kissing my chest and my fear was transformed into desire.

Just like that!

I attempted to encircle whoever it was within my arms, to gain some semblance of being the aggressor, and by doing so reclaim my masculinity, which had been so absent only moments before.

The other party didn't want to be encircled and her hands pinned my wrists to the bed as her lips touched mine, more like Eskimos touching than passion. Her long hair was against my face and I said, "Eleanor, for God's sake," and thought, I will not take your brother's leavings.

128

That's what I thought, but my flesh betrayed me and I lay back and surrendered to whatever it was she had in mind.

That's precisely what she wanted: for me to lie back. The choreography would be strictly hers. How like a Caeser, I thought.

I wish that I could compare my feelings at that moment to some other feelings, but they didn't exist in my memory. My data bank was pretty puny in that area. I lay with my arms across my eyes and let the tide of her unbelievably soft lips sweep me under and away.

It was as if she had no teeth! I felt like I was being sucked under into wet softness. The world was without foundation or structure and I was a sea creature slipping into some softer sea creature under the sea.

There was no particular rhythm to her ministrations, but there was a knowing spontaneity. The suction, the pressure, remained constant, and slowly I drove my hips up to meet it. She backed off slightly; she would remain in control.

It built, beginning in my toes, which turned up and toward me, and then into my thighs and into my manhood and into my brain. I began wailing, as if I was saying a prayer never before recited, and all the tension, the fear, and the mystery coalesced into an emotional projectile—I was the projectile—and with a half-scream, half-sigh I stormed upward into exquisite nothingness.

My hands had become entangled in her hair; my fingers were kneading her skull. I opened them and let her fall away, and only then did she sit up on her haunches like an animal that has just fed and stared down at me in the darkness.

She patted my face like a mother patting a baby's bottom, and I, returning to reality, was astonished at her gentleness.

I felt emptied for the first time since I had come to their island. My stomach and my chest felt light, as if I had given up a heavy burden. "You were wonderful," I whispered, and her hand lay against my cheek and I covered it with my own. I was so grateful!

Her dark shadow got up from the bed and went to the door, where she stood for a moment. Then she turned back toward me as if she wanted to say something, but she said nothing and she was gone the way a dream goes.

Oh Eleanor, I thought. And I slept.

Justin stood before the clock in the music room, hands locked behind his back, like some old European professor out on a walk. He didn't even turn to greet me but stared intensely at the clock as it began to chime "La Donna Mobilé."

"Wow!" I exclaimed, and he smiled at me. "Well? How did the great escape go?"

"The great what?"

"Escape from the Caesers," he announced, as if he was introducing one of those old-time melodramas, naturally with appropriate music underneath.

"I would hardly . . ." I started to explain.

He waved me off. "I understand, truly I do! We're like rich food: A person just needs to eat a sandwich once in a while."

"That's it exactly," I said, as though he'd stumbled on some philosophic truth.

He laughed with pleasure, and at that moment I came to the decision that from then on, until I had accomplished my as-yet-unformed plan, I would give him and all his family exactly what they wanted.

"You're doing just fine. The best," he said.

"I am?"

"Absolutely."

"May I respectfully ask what it is I'm doing?" I said.

"Do you really want to know? Okay. Take last night. My sister said we'd never see you again. That you would flee us. My mother agreed with her. My father thought you would come back and I knew you would! People do tend to . . . well, flee us. We are a bit much. We know that for the most part we will always be separate and apart from others. Our wealth always becomes a moat and the drawbridge is always up, whether we planned it that way or not. And then"—suddenly from the piano came a plaintive melody, something out there, by itself—"and then, we are different in other ways. Ways that do not make for the good old American melting pot. Our kind of wealth has done some things to us. No doubt. We accept it. We are not like other people."

Then, the music continuing its solitary journey, he said no more. I found myself whispering, feeling that I might never have another chance to get some questions answered, answers that I knew for certain I had to have. "How?"

He never looked up, but the song changed to a kind of heavy dark melody—a dirge or a memorial to someone or something. "All in good time," he said.

"But," I began, when the door opened and Eleanor stood there, hands on hips, full lips in a pout that you wanted to bite away. Her trousers were a brown wool tweed with a gray, yellow, and maroon plaid pattern; her yellow, collared cardigan sweater buttoned up the front. There was a paisley cravat folded under it about her neck, and over this she wore a maroon velvet blazer with gold buttons. So gorgeous was she that I found myself holding my breath and Justin watched me with a smile of approval on his face. There was an electricity about her that crackled like lightning shooting across the sky. I remembered the previous evening and put my hands in my trouser pocket. Her effect was instant. Her power didn't build; it was there from the moment she entered.

"I'm bored," she said, "and want to walk on the beach."

"So walk," her brother said.

She stamped a brown alligator loafer. "I want company."

"Count me out," Justin said. "Or haven't you noticed it's snowing?"

"We won't melt. I'll keep us warm. Do you believe I can do that?" She was directing the question at me.

"I believe anything you say," I said. Face it, the woman had me in her palm, or mouth. She could have had any man that way. My desire was not unique.

"Sit down there in the corner until we're finished and then my smitten friend can join you in your freezing trek across Antarctica."

She did as he said and we got on with our work.

TWENTY-SEVEN

There was no wind, but the snowflakes were sausage thick and hurt when they made contact with your face. Her gloved hand was in mine and we found the beach, white as bleached bone, and walked along it.

"Do you like us?" she asked, looking up at me. I stared at her. Their need for affirmation was overwhelming. "There, you don't! I can see it in your face. No one likes us."

"Of course I like you. All of you. Especially you."

"Well, you better. That's for sure."

"Oh?" I said.

"My father believes I'm falling in love with you."

"My compliments to your father," I said.

"My father is the smartest man in the world. The Caesers have to be."

"I'm sure he is," I said.

"My mother definitely knows but she's not saying. She can see into the future, you know?"

"So I understand."

She stopped. "You think we're crazy."

"No. Different."

"We are survivors."

"What exactly have you had to survive, the IRS?"

"Persecution. Through the ages. People have wanted to do away with us. Everyone has wanted to kill the Caesers and some have come very close to accomplishing it."

"Eleanor. Someplace along this beach, you've left me. I have no earthly idea what you're talking about. Why would anybody want to do you all harm? For your money?"

"Well, that certainly has brought out the most despicable jealousy, though why it has, I can't fathom. We give as much to charity as the Rockefellers and we certainly stay to ourselves. We're hardly in competition with anyone."

"I'm sorry, I don't understand."

"But how could you?" She squeezed my hand and I returned the gesture.

"Why exactly have the Caesers been persecuted through the ages? That's rather a long time."

"Because we are different."

"Eccentric, no doubt. But that would hardly bring the death penalty. Hell, if that were so, everybody in show business would be long dead."

"It has, believe me, it has. Some of our ancestors were murdered brutally. And not just by crazed mobs. Oh, no. Sometimes governments have killed us."

"This is a pointless conversation because you're not going to tell me anything," I said.

"You're angry!"

"I guess all those hints and allusions do get to me. You are taking me to the precipice and then stepping back. It confuses me and I don't like the feeling."

"I like you when you're angry. It gives you character. Let's stop here and kiss."

"Better not. Listen, the wind's come up. Sounds like screaming."

"That's not how screaming sounds at all," she said.

Now I felt cold inside, like that bitter wind, and biting cold and her words had worked their way beneath my heavy clothing and into my soul.

"You're shaking," she said, and pressed herself against me and found my lips with hers. "You're holding back," she said. "What's the matter?"

"The cold," I lied.

She began screaming high up in her head like an over-the-hill tenor trying to screech his way into one of those *William Tell* arias. "Stop!" I shouted, frightened to death.

"That's how real screaming sounds." She smiled. "Now let me demonstrate how real kissing feels."

You did last night, I thought, as her tongue forced its way into my mouth and hunted around like a finger in a jar of peanut butter.

At last we broke away. Of course I was affected. She glanced down at the evidence. "Well, I'm glad to know. I was beginning to have doubts."

"You are driving me crazy," I said over the wind.

"That's what poor Timothy used to say," she said with a laugh, then turned and began running down the beach. At last she stopped and waited for me, hands on her hips, jet black hair tossing in the wind like bats out of a cave at sunset.

"Be tender with me," she said.

"Be tender with me," I said.

"You like me?"

"My God yes."

"Love?"

"A little time," I said.

"Time? Did you say time? Well I don't know about time," she said, and I couldn't tell whether she was teasing me.

"What in hell do you want? What am I supposed to say? To do?"

"I believe"—she paused and seemed to be searching for the way to express what she meant—"I believe I want you while I can have you." She seemed amused and sad all at the same time. I didn't like the drift of her words.

"Well, I'm glad you're realistic," I said. "In the not-too-distant future, Justin and I will wind up our work here and then it's off to New York."

"Oh, I can't let you leave. I'll be alone."

"You'll have the family," I said, thinking of her and Justin in bed.

"That's not the same," she said, and I had the feeling that she knew precisely to what I was alluding.

"You can always come to New York," I said.

"Yuck," she said, that perfect nose turning up. "I studied painting in New York. It has no appeal for me. It's nothing but foreigners, you know."

"I can't believe you were lonely."

"Hardly. Justin was at Julliard and we lived together at the Plaza. We own an apartment there. You would like it. It looks down on Central Park. In the winter, it looks like a Christmas card. In the summer, it's filled with vendors," she said, giggling.

"Everybody can't be a Caeser," I said.

"Nobody can. That's the problem, don't you see?"

TWENTY-EIGHT

So here we sat prior to dinner, minus Mr. Caeser, who, Justin informed me, with all the family nodding in agreement, was involved in a very important matter. The Louis Roederer Cristal flowed as we sat staring at the flames in that gigantic fireplace or looked out at the starless night punctuated by sleet.

Eleanor, never more voluptuous, was in an emerald green velvet formal-length gown with some kind of luxuriant dark feathered sleeves. She was so curvy, it was shameless; she smiled, acknowledging my attention. It was impossible not to look at her and she seemed hungry for the attention she drew. I knew that never again in my life would I know another Eleanor. I had no doubt that she was the world's most beautiful woman, which made her need for constant reaffirmation all the more mysterious.

Mr. Caeser lumbered in, face glum, looking as if he was dragging up the tail end of a funeral procession. He sagged into a chair and Kingsley quickly filled his glass. He gulped down the contents, then held out the glass in one practiced motion for a refill. The family quickly gathered about him and there followed some kind of cryptic dialogue that sounded like a parlor game or a quiz show on television.

Justin asked, "Montervallaci?"

"Dead. Died jogging. Always in excellent health, but there you are," Mr. Caeser said.

"His son, what's his name, Riggerio?" Justin asked.

"Not interested, thank you. A fop or worse. Probably a poof. Nothing like the old man," Mr. Caeser said.

Eleanor said, "What about the Greek? The greedy Greek. He solicited us enough times. That one!"

"Not no, but hell no. He cursed; can you imagine? Terrified. Courage, the lost art. It's gone like the tango." Mr. Caeser sighed.

"And the German? Frau Helmut?" Mrs. Caeser asked.

"She was gracious, so much so, I had hopes. Alas, Frau Helmut is too old. And too rich." Mr. Caeser shook his head mournfully.

"So where exactly are we?" Mrs. Caeser asked.

"I am awaiting two more calls. One from New York," Mr. Caeser said, but there was not much hope in his voice.

"Not Harlem! Not me!" said Eleanor, her pretty face displaying disgust.

"Sometimes even the Caesers must compromise," Mr. Caeser said, lifting his glass for another hit.

"Not me. No way. Count me out. I won't even consider it!" Eleanor shouted.

"You're shouting, dear," Mrs. Caeser said.

"There's always Taiwan," Mr. Caeser said. "Though God knows it's not my favorite by far."

"They are tough," Justin said clinically. The family nodded. They disagreed about very little and I wondered what they were talking about. And then, they were all looking at me, as if I had been selected in a game of tag.

"Dear boy," Mr. Caeser said, as though he was suddenly aware of my presence. "Dear, dear boy."

I gave Mrs. Caeser her gift with an inane, "With my appreciation."

She tore it open and there followed one of the strangest scenes that I had witnessed thus far on that island. They gathered about my five-dollar handkerchief as if I had presented Mrs. Caeser with an original Rembrandt, extolling its virtues beyond imagination. The color—white—was perfect, the texture exquisite. Mr. Caeser actually dabbed at his eyes as though overcome with emotion as Eleanor kissed my lips and Justin pumped my hand with enthusiasm. Mrs. Caeser sat with a look of triumph that I could not fathom.

"You are quite simply one of us. I love this boy. I would adopt him in a moment," Mr. Caeser said as they applauded and hugged me to them.

There was something ominous about Eleanor's toast. "I hope we never lose him."

Mrs. Caeser gave me no comfort. "Only the future will tell that."

I wondered whether I'd missed some part of the conversation. They had this habit of speaking right through you, as if you weren't there at all. It was disconcerting and insulting. It wasn't as if I were deaf. At the same time, I really don't believe they realized how rude they were. I had to face it: Everything about the Caesers was bizarre.

We adjourned to the table, where the servants trooped in with the evening's pleasures. Christ, I was beginning to think like them! I laughed to myself. The evening's pleasures. Talk that way around my CPA father and he'd institute interdiction procedures immediately.

I chose not to examine the meat course. All I know is that it shimmered in a dark gravy surrounded with truffles and mushrooms, the sight of which set them to smacking their lips and making those turtledove cooing sounds in the upper register.

Naturally, all conversation ceased as they dove in. I noted that the longer I was in their presence, the worse manners became as they dropped all pretenses over their food. Nothing, nothing on earth was more important to the Caesers. I do believe that if one of them had keeled over with a heart attack, the rest would have tended to the victim only after they had finished eating.

I wondered whether at some time in their lives, or in

their family history, they had gone through a period of starvation. Something had traumatized them for certain.

Then they went into their comas, with Kingsley hovering over them as though on guard. I sat looking down at my plate. I found the whole thing not only peculiar but embarrassing.

When they came out of it, Mr. Caeser, dabbing at his wet beard with a napkin, said, "Justin tells me you went into Grace."

"Yessir."

"Your impression?"

"It was just a place. People. Ordinary people."

"You disappoint me, sir. I expected more."

"He's not Einstein," Eleanor said. "But he's cute. I love his unruly hair."

Justin asked, "What did you expect, Father? What could he pick up in a couple of hours?"

"Don't fool yourselves," Mrs. Caeser said. "This one misses nothing. To underestimate him would be foolish."

I wondered whether she was complimenting me.

"Did the good citizens of Grace appear happy?" Mr. Caeser asked, casting a sidelong glance at his wife.

"Well yes, I suppose so," I said, having no memory whatever of anyone in Grace answering to that description.

"We look upon them as our extended family. Our children," Mr. Caeser said, a benevolent smile about his lips.

"Did you know that every high school graduate in Grace receives a full four-year scholarship to the college of his choice? We've done it forever," Justin said, and it didn't sound as if he was bragging, just stating a fact.

"That's remarkable and wonderful," I said.

"We also pay for the clinic," Mrs. Caeser said.

"And the elderly get regular monthly checks," Eleanor said.

"What lucky people," I said.

"We love them," Mrs. Caeser said.

"And when they're bad?" I asked, smiling as if my question was a joke.

"Why we spank them, we spank them good," Eleanor said, and just to prove that wasn't all bad, she squeezed me gently between the legs.

"Very few of them step out of line," Mr. Caeser said. I believed it.

"Just what would constitute stepping out of line?" I asked.

"Mundane errors. Certainly nothing big. Like curiosity. That would surely be a sin," Mr. Caeser said.

"About?"

"This family. Us. This island. This home. Our privacy is sacred; we pay handsomely for it. Call it an idiosyncrasy. We require it in great measure. You do understand?" Mr. Caeser asked.

"Yes, of course," I said. I was becoming an infamous liar and getting better at it all the time. It was a new habit for me. I had always been outspoken and honest to the point of fault.

"He's fabricating," Mrs. Caeser said. The family smiled as though that was an accomplishment, too.

I blushed but defended myself. "No, really I'm not." By now my penis was out and in Eleanor's practiced hand. I would have agreed to anything.

"You're off this time, Mother." Justin came to my defense. "I believe he's, er, preoccupied. Eleanor, as usual, has no sense of timing."

She gave me a final squeeze and removed her hand. I sat there holding my breath and trying not to ejaculate. "We who treasure privacy must, in some measure, give it to others," Eleanor said with a sly laugh.

Her father saluted her. "It's the American way!" And now my flag, at last at quarter mast, could be slipped back into my trousers.

"Now then, gentlemen," said Mr. Caeser, "tomorrow

140

evening after dinner we shall retire to the music room, where I expect to hear the results of your labors."

"We're not ready," Justin protested, but he might as well have been protesting the snow. Mr. Caeser brushed him away as one might brush away a bothersome mosquito. "Tomorrow evening."

Mrs. Caeser suddenly changed the subject. "Have you anyone else to try?"

Mr. Caeser's face took on a grave look. "One, a gentleman out of Chicago. Mr. Ladislaw Kochinka. Highly recommended. In fact, that accursed Kalil, damn his soul wherever he may be, spoke rather well of him. I've established contact and he swore he would get back to me by the end of the week. Until then, having no immediate choice, we'll hope and wait."

Mrs. Caeser persisted. "And if he says no, what then?"

You could have heard a pin drop. Everyone stared at Mr. Caeser. Even I, who had no idea what they were talking about, felt the tension. I was certain of only one thing: Whatever it was, it was illegal. Why did I feel the beginnings of fear?

Mr. Caeser sighed. "Then we will do what we have to do. The Caesers must go on and we shall. A toast to that. Come come, young man, lift your glass. You do want the Caesers to endure? No matter what, eh? Go on, say it. Favor an old man with a few words."

The family, glasses lifted, were looking at me, awaiting some accursed word. I had been given an order I didn't understand. "Say what?"

As though teaching a child the alphabet, Mr. Caeser said, "I want the Caesers to go on."

I thought, I want the Caesers to go to hell. I said, "I want the Caesers to go on."

Mr. Caeser looked from me to them in ugly triumph.

I could not get to sleep. I had arranged the pillows—I slept with three—into every geometric pattern and anatomical combination. I had tried the magic word *hemlock,* which an article I once had read swore was an ancient surefire method of getting to sleep. However, tried-and-true *hemlock* wasn't having any effect that evening, nor was the champagne and wine I had consumed.

I bunched the pillows beneath my head and, with an arm over my eyes, accepted my mother's counsel. That she was right about 40 percent of the time was an astonishing achievement to me, who was almost never right. Her theory: You cannot sleep because your mind is busy trying to sort life out. Ergo, unsort and you will relax and absolutely sleep.

Now what was keeping me awake? Food? I hadn't eaten more than usual that evening. Champagne, wine? No way, these usually acted upon me as sedatives. Sex? Unrequited sex? Eleanor had stopped her tender ministrations prior to my climaxing. True. My mind was not on sex, however. The peculiar behavior of the Caesers? Hell, that was the norm. They were no more odd that evening than at any other time. Their behavior did not fluctuate. They were always crazy. Something specifically said that evening? No. Hints, veiled threats: I was used to them.

How about the prospect of performing our show? A possibility, that. It excited me and I could hardly wait. I had absolute confidence in our work.

Go back, further back, I told myself. The village. Grace. Something stirred in me and instead of relaxing, I felt something, a part of my brain waving frantically like a tipsy semaphore. What in the village? Miss Polly, town pharmacist, drunken Miss Polly with her Ancient Mariner's tale of lost L.C. Tragic face-split-in-half L.C. I shuddered and saw his face, which, of course, I had never seen and never would see.

Yet it was L.C. prodding me, waving to me from some dark street, urging me to come on, teasing me, daring me to continue my thought process. L.C., peeping out from some corner, then ducking out of sight, then peeping out again. This was ridiculous! Vietnam mass-produced L.C.'s like cars off an assembly line. What did L.C. have to do with me? Yet in my head, in my being, he had come to life. I saw him sitting at a silent piano, giving soundless bird whistles to birds that weren't there. "Goddammit," I said aloud, in frustration, and turned on my side, putting one pillow between my legs.

Am I trying to say that I was being visited by L.C.'s spirit? No. I do not believe in any of that. It was, I believe, electronic impulses bouncing off barriers in my brain like a pinball machine. Lights flashing on and off but mostly *TILT!*

My mother's counsel. Be very basic. What did L.C. mean to Marion Anderson? Not the man, the name. Lafcadio Charles. Lafcadio was the first name of a southern writer. Charles was the heir to the British throne. Nothing there. L.C. was a kid I had gone to grammar school with, the ringmaster in the circus we put on in the second grade. L.C. Greenwood was a great pro-football player for Pittsburgh. Beyond that . . . wait, wait a minute. I had heard those initials, seen them, some other place. Where?

I turned over on my stomach, the pillow now under my belly. Mercifully, I was getting sleepy. Thank you, Mother. My eyelids were heavy and my breathing slowed its pace as my body prepared for sleep.

Then I sat up as if I'd been hit with an electric shock and my teeth began chattering—I could hear them—and my toes and the tip of my nose began to freeze and the hair on my arms stood at attention.

I remembered.

Packages of meat in Justin's freezer at school. They had been labeled L.C. What had he said? He had said something, because I remembered asking him. I remembered his answer. I could hear it. "L.C. is the code of a particular herd in Argentina."

Again I was on my back, arms rigid by my side, like a mortician had just finished with me. I willed my mind to be blank because I did not feel that it could deal with emerging truth. I was as exhausted as if I had run a marathon and I felt my pulse racing in my veins. Suddenly, my mouth was dry, as if one of those dental pumps had sucked all the moisture out, and my tongue became leaden. I am certain that I could not have spoken.

Despite my efforts, words popped up in my head like numbers in the little window of a cash register. Caesers. *Sale*. L.C. *Sale*. Cannibals. That one stayed in the window.

Then there came over me overwhelming sadness and I felt as if I was crying, but inside, because my lips were pressed shut in silence. For their victims. For L.C., whom I'd known only through the drunken dissertation of his sister, who was surely a victim, too. Timothy. I knew Timothy and not through anyone else's words. He had been flesh and blood before . . . before he was just flesh. Poor Timothy they called him; hell, I called him that. Oh yes, he was poor all right; he had come to this accursed place and fallen into the clutches of monsters.

The dam opened and I began to sob aloud and I knew for whom I was sobbing. What had Mrs. Caeser so slyly labeled me? Poor Marion. I was poor Marion; the name was mine, like it or not, bestowed by a Caeser as a king bestowed knighthood.

Who else was on their grocery list when there was no L.C., no Timothy, and no—I shuddered so hard the bed shook—and no me?

I knew why they had had so few guests—a new name to call food—on their island. What had they eaten before, after, in between? How many meals was a human carcass good for? I knew nothing about such things, but who did but the Caesers? And how did they get that way? How long had they been carrying on this obscenity?

They had to have a supply, no, not a supply, a supplier! Of course. Evil-looking Mr. Kalil, he had to have been it before he bailed out on them, Interpol hot on his bloody trail.

What a profession, I thought. I'd just bet that would get my father to lower his *Journal* and maybe even put that rotten pipe down! Mr. Kalil, purveyor by appointment, to their Majesties the Caesers! Trumpet music. Wow.

Now they were busy searching for a new one, a professional human butcher who could take care of their little addiction.

Well, why not? What was not deliverable in our times? If you had the money to pay for it. I remembered a buddy bragging about what his visit to Las Vegas was like. "Say you want a slice of watermelon at three in the morning. Pick up the phone and order it! Say you want a woman, call the bell captain! You just order what you want!"

Weren't young "chickens" supplied to pedophiliacs? Dope to addicts? Snuff films to people who could get off only by watching other people die? Pre-operative transexuals? There's a phone number in *Screw* magazine. Women's clothes for men? There are boutiques that sell them. Everything, everything was available if you had the money, and boy oh boy, did the Caesers have the money!

When was Marion scheduled for the menu? When was I going to tragically walk into the ocean, fall off a cliff, have a heart attack? They controlled their world and they could do anything.

I sat up in bed. Lying back had suddenly become all too symbolic of a coward, a victim awaiting his turn, and while I was no Sergeant York, I was no coward.

Or at least I didn't think so.

Yet I had never won a fight, from the school bully who had broken my nose to the piano mover who had dropped my Baldwin and then had answered my anger with a black eye. But I had fought on, gotten up off the floor, and ineffectualy flailed away until I was beaten into submission. Beatings made me neither quake nor quiver. I was certain there was a law of averages that would catch up to me, and in my life I would win a fight or two.

On the other hand, I had never fought for my life.

What to do? Flee the island came first to mind. And then what? Spend the rest of my life trying not to see the yellow streak down my back? How would I feel about myself? I was awfully young to acknowledge my cowardice and the thought of a lifetime knowing it made me feel awful.

Could I go to the authorities? Now I'm standing in a cramped office . . . an overweight detective with a cigar butt in his mouth, bored, waiting to hear my complaint, the hundredth of his day. Through his smoke, "What is it?"

I blurt out, "I want to report a cannibal."

This guy who's heard it all asks, "Proof?"

I didn't have any. L.C.? Everybody, including his sister—particularly his sister—knew he was mentally ill. Would she or anybody else in Grace testify against the Caesers? I didn't think so. They were all afraid and I didn't blame them. Timothy? *Corpus delicti,* please. I would bet there wasn't a skeleton lying around. Mr. Kalil? Was that even his real name? Did he tell the Caesers a true story? Was Interpol even aware of his existence? He appeared to be on the lam. God, I was beginning to think like dialogue in a pulp magazine!

Yet I did believe that there was proof. The Caesers were too haughty, too cynical to spend a lot of time covering their tracks. I pushed proof away for a moment as a new consideration entered my thinking.

Suppose I got the hell off the island? Would the Caesers let me be? I had no doubt that they had the wherewithal to send after me. I did not believe that I could hide from them. No, they would get me. They would not let a loose cannon roll about the deck. The thought of spending my life in hiding held no appeal. I liked who I was. I wanted to stay me.

Back to proof. There had to be some and it had to be on this island. Could I find it? Why was I, Mr. No Coward, trembling? I was not one of the Hardy boys and though I had a trench coat exactly like Colombo's, I had neither his charm nor genius. I was no detective.

What I needed was a game plan, a methodology—like writing a musical, first the idea, then the story. I started at the end and worked backward.

What was my goal? What did I want to accomplish? Simple, that. I wanted to bring the Caesers to justice. But justice—formal, before-the-bar justice—was built for the Caesers of the world. They would have a battery of the best attorneys that money could purchase. God only knows what judges they owned outright. And know-how, generations of know-how. The Caesers had honed the skills of survival, about which I knew virtually nothing. There would be no trick, no strategy that they didn't know, and, in fact, they had probably invented some. The Caeser gambit. They were old evil.

So what would constitute justice, Caeser style?

The answer was their lifestyle: death.

If I was right, that was exactly what they deserved. But could Marion Anderson be Judge Roy Bean? Hang the bastards! Next case! It occurred to me that I was quite mad, but I chose not to fight it. If madness was the only arena in which I could meet them, I'd plunge on.

However, who had appointed me God's avenging angel? I answered that question with a question: If not me, who? Wasn't that what the Holocaust was really about? The world doing nothing in the face of evil?

I decided. The Caesers would have to die and I would have to do it. I would have to kill them. But *them* was not accurate. *Them* meant other human beings. I would have to kill evil. Having decided, I felt better—not heroic, but better.

I proceeded with a plan. First, I would have to survive long enough to accomplish my goal.

Did I have any say in the matter? Would anything I did prolong my life beyond their immediate needs? Unless, unless a relationship, a very serious relationship with Eleanor might buy me a little time. Had it bought Timothy any? "Eleanor, you is my woman now."

Eleanor and I would have to be an "item." A serious one. Marriage in the immediate future. Sir, I've come to ask for Eleanor's hand.

Justin. Good buddy Justin. Brothers, that's what we were, and collaborators. Justin and I, our names up in lights. Bro.

Mrs. Caeser. I would be the dutiful son-in-law-to-be. Long talks in the garden and little gifts. Careful of that one, damn careful, her intuition was more than a bit frightening. Mild flirtation? Hmmm.

Mr. Caeser. Oh Jesus, what did Mr. Caeser want but a good chunk of someone's buttocks in a tasty sauce? And great attention to his sermonettes. Total agreement, no matter what he said.

Advantages. I knew and they didn't know I knew. Compliments. But would that buy me time? Time to . . .

What about allies? I didn't think I could do what I had to do alone. Miss Polly, good drunken Miss Polly. How could she help? She might if I could present proof that L.C. had died at their hands. Maybe her love of her brother would be stronger than her love of drink, and her obvious fear of the family. Maybe. Worth exploring.

Annabel Lee. How involved was she? Hell, she didn't even eat the stuff. I was now calling it the stuff. Annabel Lee, a card-carrying vegetarian. Did she have any idea what was going on and would she give a damn? After all, she was a Caeser, proud of it. But did she know what being a Caeser constituted? How could she? She may as well have been dwelling on some other planet. Even the day was foreign to her. I could not fathom her reaction, assuming that I could even tell her. And what a lousy task that would be, telling Annabel Lee the truth about her family, her support system.

I wasn't sure I could do that.

I did not want her ruin on my hands.

So there I was, a goal and a dismal few possibilities of allies: a drunken pharmacist and an albino recluse. The A Team looked mighty puny.

So what else? What did Marion Anderson have going for himself? My head and a good tongue that had always served me well.

I pasted a grin on my face, lying there in the darkness, and swore never to let it slip away until I had accomplished my mission. The grin was no joke. If the family did not perceive me as a beloved fool, poor Marion's days might be very limited indeed.

Again back to how much time I had. I had seen them desperate once before without knowing what it was that had made them so. However, the next morning, poor Timothy had made his walk into the ocean.

I had to watch them very intensely. Good God, I was fighting for my life and for more. More than me. That gave me peace.

More than me.

I slept and had no dreams.

TWENTY-NINE

The music room. Justin asked whether I had been drinking. I shook my head, had no idea what he was talking about. He said, "You're high, giddy, everything's wonderful. We know that's not you."

There was a concerned smile on his face, but he was serious. I knew I had, in my amateurish efforts, overdone it and I knew I'd better be a lot more careful.

"I am high," I said, striking out boldly.

"Want to share the reason?"

"No, I don't want to. Do I have a choice?" Inside, I was thinking frantically. What did I have to be high about?

"I'm afraid not. Not on this island," he said, any semblance of warmth vanished.

"Sounds like a dictatorship," I said, begging for time, thinking, thinking, what would I be high about?

"That's exactly what it is, didn't you know? It's the price one pays for the trains running on time. Translate that to read, all the luxury, all these goodies. Now give or I'll . . ."

"Yes?"

The grin returned. "I'll huff and I'll puff and I'll blow your house down!"

Or you'll eat me up, you cannibal bastard, I thought. "Okay, you win and I've no doubt the Caesers always do," I said.

"Always, but always in good causes. We never take advantage."

"I think you'll understand why I'm a little hesitant to tell you, to tell you first," I said.

"Wait, I've got it." He crashed down on the piano with great regal chords. "Of course! What a fool I am. It's about Eleanor. Am I right? Dammit, tell me!"

"Yes," I said modestly, eyes downcast.

"And . . . go on, don't stand there like the village idiot."

"Well, Justin, the fact is, I realize I care for Eleanor, a lot more than I should."

"More than you should? You've lost me," he said.

"What I mean is, with poor Timothy just gone . . ."

He blinked. I do believe he had forgotten who Timothy was or that he had ever existed. "Oh. Certainly. Well, that's life. These things happen. Life has to go on. It's not like they were married or, God forbid, had children. Ha! A young Timothy, that's what we need here." He went off into hysterical laughter, all control lost.

"Well anyway, now you know. I'd appreciate if you didn't say anything. I don't know why, but I have the feeling Eleanor might appreciate knowing first. Notwithstanding how close you and she are."

Now there was pure evil, a dirty grin on his face. "We are very close," he said solemnly.

One good thing about conning the Caesers. They thought they knew more about everything than anyone else. It was a vulnerability that I planned to use to the maximum.

"I think it's wonderful," he said. "I can think of no one I'd be more proud to welcome into this family. My brother will be my brother-in-law."

"Hey, hold on. She may not accept me."

"So when are you going to pop the question?"

"I thought I might approach the subject when we're finished here. Eleanor said something about wanting to paint me."

A look of shock replaced the pleasure on his face. He jumped to his feet, fists clenched white. "She what? What's that?"

"Hey, calm down. She doesn't want to kill me; she wants to paint me!" I blurted out.

"Greedy, greedy, greedy," he said, quivering with rage. I spotted a bust of Haydn with which I was going to crack his head if he came at me. However, it was not me at whom his anger was directed. "How dare she? Does my father know?"

"Cool it, Justin, before you have a stroke. Does your father know what?"

"That Eleanor wants to paint you?" he roared, leaning across the piano. His breath was sweet and cloying, as if he'd been chewing a sour mint.

"How the hell would I know? Look, there was a note under my door when I woke up. Here. Read it. I will.

'When you and Justin are finished today, come to my studio. I want to sketch you!' That's all."

He unwound immediately. Now the maniac was smiling, resuming his seat on the piano bench. "Oh. Oh! She just wants to sketch you. I'm sorry. I was wrong. You do see, don't you?"

"I can't say that I do, but I can't see that it makes any difference."

"Of course it doesn't," he said. "None at all!"

"Just old me," I said, tapping at her studio door.

"Come in!" she called out.

She wore slim-cut jeans and a matching jacket decorated with metal studs and leather fringe.

She stood before an empty canvas, a charcoal stick in hand. "You sit there," she said, pointing to a high stool. The ceiling window was open and gray snow fell from a gray sky. "Now relax," she said, "this isn't an execution."

"I'm glad," I said. "I love life."

"You do?" she asked, turning my face slightly to the left with long, cool fingers. "I am full of love," I said, looking her straight in the eyes.

"You," she said, beginning to sketch, "are full of bull." I didn't like that. While it was true, a lot depended on my ability to be believable—an ability that I was certain I possessed in abundance.

"I've been doing a lot of thinking," I said. "About us. As in you and me."

She continued with her work as if I hadn't said anything. "Am I disturbing you?" I asked.

"I'm listening. I'm all ears."

"You're all loveliness," I said. "Now where was I?"

She liked that and gave me the finger with a free hand.

"Make my eyes green," I said. "I have always wanted green eyes."

"No can do. The finished work will be you, and sorry,

you don't have green eyes. You have brown eyes. Dull, trusting, brown eyes."

"I can see that imperfections drive you batty," I said.

"Of course. I want everyone to be like me. Perfect."

"Mmmmm," I muttered.

I knew my silent comment would irritate her. The Caesers, the most mysterious of people, would not tolerate it in others.

"That sound, that ridiculous *mmmmm*, what was it supposed to mean?" she asked, erasing a line on the canvas, swiftly replacing it with another.

"You are perfect," I said.

"Yes. That's more like it. Well, don't just sit there like a goose. You are a lyricist, aren't you? Or at least Justin says you are. How perfect?"

"You're not real. You're every man's fantasy, one that can't possibly come true. And then, there you are! And it is true. There is perfection. It does exist. And it's frightening," I said.

"Frightening?" She was nibbling on a red bottom lip with perfect little white pearl teeth.

"It's a theory of mine. We men should never confront our dreams or they'll drive us mad."

"Crazy?"

"Yes," I said.

"Hold still. And are you?"

"Am I what?" I teased.

"Mad."

"Hopelessly. Over you," I said. She laid the charcoal down and undulated her way to me. She cupped my face in her hands. I was thinking of a fishing line, still in the water.

"Don't play with me," she said. "That would be bad for both of us, terrible for you."

"I love you, Eleanor," I said. The line began to quiver.

"Yes. I believe you do." She kissed me with a tenderness

that I did not know she possessed. Got you, I thought. "You know you don't have to talk about love. I want to go to bed with you."

"I want that, too. But more. I want you forever." I enfolded her in my arms, my face in raven hair.

She pulled back, studied me gravely. "Are you proposing?"

"Yes," I said, holding my breath. Now the line bobbed.

"I love you, too," she said. Got'cha, I thought. "You'll have to talk to my father."

That stopped me. I was frightened of the man and doubted my ability to fool him. I was certain there was nothing he had not experienced and, when necessary, sat in judgment on. I knew that he and his brood had survived not only by their wealth but by their ability to sniff danger, any danger. I wonder whether she thought I shivered out of passion.

"I, er, am frightened of your father," I said. Sometimes the truth is useful.

"Most people are. He's a very gentle man. Unless . . . you cross him," she said, and we had a good laugh at that, hers easy and true, mine faked and forced. "He's probably in the library."

"Tomorrow," I said. "I need a little time to gather my courage."

"You are a 'fraidy cat," she said. "I like that. People who are afraid do better with the Caesers. Don't ask me why, but it's true!"

I wanted to slap her lovely face, to shout, You bitch! I kissed her.

THIRTY

A couple of new facets at dinner that evening. My Eleanor had undergone the amazing transformation from vixen to Miss Prim and Proper.

I casually dropped my hand on her leg beneath the table and she pinched it and said, in a voice I thought could be heard in the neighboring county, "Please don't."

I stared at her and she smiled back, a serene, wifely smile. I shook my head. I didn't believe it. Justin winked at me as though to say, It's a brand new ball game, buddy boy. Buddy boy gave a weak wink in return and stirred his leek soup.

The wonderfully consistent thing about the Caesers was their inconsistency. Every moment with them was different and unpredictable—except when it came to their eating habits. That remained constant as each of them retreated into his or her tiny envelope of private pleasure. Private love sounds. Meat was for them an adored, precious, living thing; it had life even on the platter. I would not have been surprised if they spoke aloud to it!

After we ate, and they took their little naps, we slowly followed Mr. Caeser into the music room for the command performance.

I thought he might cancel it. His mind seemed elsewhere; he kept removing his pocket watch and studying it, the family's eyes on him and it. I asked Mr. Caeser whether I might see him the next day. He barely nodded, in a disconcerted manner.

I stood in the bow of the piano as narrator and performer.

Just as I began to set the scene, I saw the door open a crack. Annabel Lee was in secret attendance. It was so sad. I aimed all the love songs at that barely opened door.

The Caesers were a surprisingly good audience, laughing at all the jokes, applauding all the songs. And all in the right places!

Their pride in Justin was obvious as they beamed his way. They knew music! They were almost as enthused over it as they were over meat, surely the highest accolade they could bestow.

Nor were they less hip to my lyrics. When I turned a particularly good phrase or inserted one of those clever rhymes six or seven lines later, they applauded or laughed. It was stupid of me to be surprised at their worldliness; there was probably nothing this family had not experienced many times over.

The moment was pure magic and when I descended from that particular heaven reserved for those who create and share their creativity with an appreciative audience, I blinked in confusion, my palms sweaty. Then I remembered just who my audience was and the magic left me; reality set in.

We ended our show with my saying, "To be continued next act!" More applause, and Eleanor pushed her chair back and rushed up. I held out my arms to her but she whizzed by and embraced her brother. I stared at them as they held a kiss, until I realized that Mrs. Caeser was tugging at my arm. Then she took my face between her hands and kissed me and shoved her very active tongue down my throat. I almost fainted and hoped that motherly hand was hiding us from view. She drew back, eyes blazing, and said, "I'm going to reward your genius." I gulped.

Mr. Caeser left his son's embrace—they were so emotional, while I had no memory of ever doing anything but shaking my father's hand, and with not too much enthusiasm on his part, as if he suspected that our shake was a prelude to a favor—and hugged me to him in a hold that almost drove the breath from my body. This was a very powerful man.

He said, "We owe you much, young man. I always knew my son was a composer, possibly even a great composer, but were it not for you, the world would never know!"

"It is I who is fortunate, sir."

He held a fat finger to his lips, shushing me. "We Caesers know us. Had you not reached out to my son, or at any rate to his talent, and I submit they are one and the same, that would have been the end of it, except for his playing for us on evenings like this. You see we Caesers simply can't reach out. We never know who is on the other side. You do understand?"

"You mean people after your wealth?"

"Oh yes, to be sure! But worse. Far worse. You wouldn't believe it." He looked about furtively as if he was checking against strangers, and said, "There have been those who have even sought our destruction. Look at me, young man. Is that doubt I read in your eyes? Do you take my words for the prattling of an old man?"

"Oh, no sir! Not at all. It's just that I find this family so, well, noble, that I can't even imagine anyone wishing you harm." Would he buy that? I doubted it. It was so patently fraudulent.

He did buy it, however. These people adored compliments. Tears rolled from his small evil eyes. "Yes, yes, noble. Your way with the king's English does not fail you. We are a noble, if misunderstood, flock. Our history is written in our own blood. Mankind has never understood the Caesers."

He squeezed my shoulders and Eleanor gave me a peck on the cheek, as if I might be carrying a social disease. I looked at her quizzically, but that glorious face was an expressionless mask.

Mr. Caeser addressed us as if he were speaking from a balcony. "I am convinced that there is real talent at work, talent that deserves its moment. Justin, when you and your friend give the word, I am prepared to do whatever is necessary toward that end."

Now Justin and I pumped hands feverishly and our happy little band retired for the evening.

My secret magician was performing her trick upon me again. I was a willing subject. The excitement of performing that evening filled me with tension that was near the bursting point. My hand, in her hair, established the exquisite rhythm.

Surely this was the ultimate luxury, all those sensations requiring nothing of me but that I lie there and give myself up. Oh but I wanted to see my Eleanor! That gorgeous face, that Caeser, devouring me! I stopped. What was I thinking?

I reached over and flicked on the table light, holding her head in place with my other hand. Annabel Lee looked up at me, hand over mouth, dark pits of her eyes boring through mine.

"Well I'll be!" I gasped.

"How could you? You've ruined everything," she said sadly.

"The hell I have," I said, pointing to my still-evident excitement. "Everything's the same."

"Put it away," she said. "I find you disgusting." She sounded exactly like Eleanor.

I did as she asked. "Annabel, please try to understand. Life can't be lived in the darkness. It reduces everything to secrets, furtiveness."

"Mine can," she said.

"Okay. Yours. But my life is also involved. You don't inhabit this world alone. Besides, it really isn't necessary."

"I am a freak! Who wants a freak except a sideshow?" she shouted.

"Oh, Annabel Lee. Come here," I said, and tugged her up until she was lying in my arms. I patted her like you'd pat a frightened animal. I turned my face to hers.

"Please turn out that light," she said.

1 5 8

"No," I said, "from now on, light."

She tried to wrench away but I held her until she ceased struggling. "Listen to me just this one time. Then do what you please. I promise this is the only sermon I'll ever deliver to you. Okay? Will you listen?" I asked.

"Yes," she whispered. "But don't be cruel. I can't handle that."

"Cruel? How cruel? Is the truth cruel if it's told for good reason? I'm asking because I don't know, either. You are hiding from life, from pleasure. You live in the darkness, and for bats that's okay, but not for human beings. People do not hide, particularly if they've done nothing to justify it. And you haven't. You got born. Period. Blind people get along in the real world, blind people with dogs and white canes. People in wheelchairs get along and retarded people get along. They do not hide. You hide. Know why? You hide because you can. That money says you can spend your life avoiding life."

"They'll stare at me. I'd die."

"Probably. It would be brutal, sure. But after a while, I don't believe you'd notice or even give a damn. You'd be out of your prison and on with your life. A real life. Am I making any sense?"

"Nothing you're saying is new. Don't you think I've thought of it, all of it, in the beginning over and over? Of course I have. I am a thinking creature. My insides are the same as yours. Just the outside's different."

"Okay, so you know it," I said. "Good. Great. But is that it? Does it just stop there? You may as well occupy a coffin. You are not living life. That may be the greatest of all sins."

"It's too late. If I had tried sooner, but now . . ."

"I'm sorry you feel that way. I only wanted to help."

"You are a nice man." She got up from the bed and went toward the door. It was now or never.

"Annabel Lee, can we talk for a moment?"

159

"We have talked."

"It's about, it's about something else. Please come back. Here, sit here."

"What is it?"

"It's, well, I don't know exactly how to say it, or even if I should."

"You are being mysterious. I don't like you that way."

"You see, I'm frightened. I have suspicions that frighten me."

She laughed but hidden in the laughter was a mild tremor of fear. "You sound like a detective on PBS."

"No. This is not a TV story. I can't turn this tube off. This is for real and, I believe, dangerous."

She looked at me incredulously, but again I had the feeling that she was attempting to bluff. "Dangerous? To whom?"

"Me. No, don't laugh. Don't do that!"

"What is it? Say it; I can't just sit here while you stammer," she said, every inch of her the imperial Caesers.

"I've got some information, crazy information; I even feel crazy saying it aloud, but that doesn't make it any less real."

Her hands were folded across her chest. "What kind of information?"

"About murder. A couple of murders, maybe more, no telling how many more. Probably mass murder."

"Please don't tell me any more." The wind had been knocked out of her. Now I knew. Annabel Lee had not lived completely in the darkness.

"I've got to tell someone and I'm sorry, but there's just you."

"Me? I'm a recluse."

I said it so softly that I wasn't even certain that I had. "It concerns the Caesers."

The white mask of her face tightened as if something were tugging her skin from behind. "What concerns the Caesers?"

"I'm losing my courage," I said.

"I believe you're psychotic and don't want to hear what you have to say," she said, but made no move to leave.

"I'm not crazy; I kind of wish I was. And you really don't think I am."

"Oh?"

"There's dread on your face."

"No. Pity. Disgust. You've ugly things to say about the Caesers. I know why! Envy, you're filled with it," she said.

"Save the pity for the victims. I'm just fine, thanks."

"Well?"

"Well what?" I asked, still playing for time.

"Say it!"

"I don't know. I don't know at all."

"Know? What are you talking about?"

"Maybe I am wrong. Maybe I'm hallucinating."

"Maybe you're lying! What's the matter, lost your nerve?"

"Yes, that's it exactly. You wouldn't believe me, anyway. And worse, I think you'd tell them."

"Right on both counts."

"Thanks just the same," I said.

"Want some advice? Advice like you gave me? Drop it."

"I don't believe I can do that. I can't just walk away from murder. Then I'd be no better than . . ."

"Say it, you bastard!" She spit it out.

"The Caesers."

She was rigid, her head slightly tilted, like a snowman who's melted at an angle. "I will tell my family. The Caesers do not betray the Caesers. You are a despicable creature who's come among us, eaten our food . . ."

"Not all your food."

"Drunk our wine, even made love to us. You are a user! Just what kind of thing are you?"

"I do not take human life. In my peon's world, that's murder, and guess what? It doesn't matter who commits it, it's still murder. A crime. The worst crime!"

"Shut up!" she screamed.

"And one other little detail. If you tell your family about this conversation, you may have murder on your hands."

"You are in need of a psychiatrist," she said.

"I am serious, deadly serious. Just keep that in mind. If you hear that I walked into the sea or suddenly disappeared, remember, you'll have been in on it and all the hiding out in your apartment won't make your participation any the less."

"You'll hear from my father about this."

"There are things going on right outside your window, Annabel Lee, bloody things."

She looked like one of those rare Siberian tigers about to pounce. She whirled around and left me alone and terrified.

THIRTY-ONE

He sat behind his great desk, one hand on the telephone, the other holding a magazine. He was in repose but tense, as if he was willing the phone to ring. I stood at the door like a soldier waiting for permission to enter.

"I like that, young man. Yours is an age that sallies forth. I despise that. There's a time, a time for everything, only we can't wait, can we?"

I knew he didn't expect an answer. I nodded enthusiastically.

"So in we bluster, in we blunder, spilling the milk, knocking china to the floor. We are a generation of blustering bulls wreaking havoc in the china shop. But, I must say, not you. I congratulate not only you but those who imparted to you that splendid quality of waiting, of being able to wait. Now then, don't stand there, enter and sit down and have a bit of port. You are drinking 1734 vintage port, Cockburn. Hmmm, not bad I'd say." He peered at me over the rim of his glass.

"Sir, I've come to, well, to speak with you."

"Relax, lad. The giant doesn't bite." He repeated it to himself and began laughing, his big head thrown back. You could see the laughter rumbling up from his belly. I smiled wanly. "Now then, out with it, on with it!"

"It's about Eleanor."

His hand left the phone to press against its mate. "Ahhhhh," he said, making the same sound he made over meat.

The man overwhelmed me. My mouth was dry.

"And what about Eleanor?" he asked, drawing the last syllable out as if his tongue had become stuck on it.

The telephone rang and his hand shot out for it, grabbed it, and pressed it into his ear. I didn't know whether to remain seated or leave. The conversation was mostly one-sided as he answered in grunts and uh-hmms. Then he stood and began to pace the room, the phone on a long extension cord. I believe he had forgotten my presence. He stalked the room like an animal.

I glanced across the expanse of the desk at the magazine he had been reading. I could have picked it up and flipped through it and he wouldn't have noticed, so deep was he in his telephone conversation.

Suddenly my testicles shrank up within me and my fingertips grew as cold as if I was holding an ice cube. It was the magazine cover—a long knife being held against a knife grinder, and in an insert, a man in a meat cutter's smock and his testimony: "The Kuppe Sharpest Wetstone Knife Grinder is the best sharpener I've used since the old-style water grinding wheel used in packinghouses way back when. My blade stays sharp and I grind less."

It was a catalogue of butcher's supplies. The old monster

had been doing a little research. Then I felt his presence behind me and I lowered my eyes and looked at my lap.

He went around the desk, returned the phone to the cradle, and sank into his chair as if he'd just done twenty laps in a pool. He poured some more port and said, "We'll see, won't we? Play it to the end. Do what we must. Not a philosophy for other men. For the Caesers, our particular circumstances, the only philosophy. Now then to Eleanor. What exactly is it?"

"Sir, I've fallen in love with Eleanor."

He sat back, hands behind his head. "You have, have you?"

I leaned forward, as if I were confessing to a priest sitting on a low bench. "I know I shouldn't have, have no right really, I mean with Timothy's recent . . ." I searched for the right word. He saved me the effort.

"Demise."

I nodded. I could not say it. He unlocked his hands and with the right one made a flicking gesture. Thus was Timothy dismissed from our discussion.

"And your intentions? Obviously, you have them, or why else see me?"

"I would like your permission to marry her."

"And have you made this known to my daughter?"

"Yessir. She said to ask you."

"Hmmm." He closed his eyes, rubbed his temple. The eyes popped open and focused on me. "You must have some idea of what marrying a Caeser entails?"

I thought, You bastard, you bet I do! "The responsibility is awesome," I said humbly.

He refilled our glasses. "There would be legal ramifications, but you expect that. A contract. We've got to protect ourselves."

"Sir, I'm not marrying Eleanor for her wealth."

He looked at me with pity. "Of course. To be sure. Love."

I lowered my eyes like a blushing handmaiden.

164

"I want to sleep on it. You do understand?"

"Of course."

"I'll tell you something in a couple of days. You despair. Don't deny it. It's written on you like Gorbachev's birthmark. Well, don't. Important matters like who becomes a Caeser are not so easily determined. You wonder why the delay? I'll tell you why. The day you marry my daughter, if you do, I will transfer the sum of ten million dollars to your account. You do have one?"

I thought of my $111.34 balance and said, "Of course." That would make it 10 million, 111 dollars, and 34 cents—a tidy sum.

"Not another dime, mind you. That's in the contract. Should the marriage not work out, you would not get another dime. The Caesers will not be taken advantage of."

"Sir, I am marrying Eleanor, should you give your permission, for . . ."

"Yes, yes, I heard you the first time," he said wearily. "Love. For poets and dreamers. Money, our kind of money, drives the sanest of men mad. Wimpy creatures become swaggering oafs in the twinkling of any ugly eye. Desires, not even whispered in the secrecy of one's own mind, become a viable possibility, a vice, taken almost casually and with inevitable sly boasts. And then what about love? A word. A sigh. A memory, a very bare one."

"I really do understand."

"Really? How could you? Now get out and let me get about this task you've given me."

"Sir?"

He swigged down a full glass of that 1734 port as if it were a Pepsi. "Oh, very well, if you must know. I am going to call a private investigator who has been in the Caeser employ for many years. That gentleman—and he is hardly that, a sneaky sort, exactly what you'd expect, though I do admit, superb at his greasy trade—will investigate you from the day you were born. Did you get a traffic ticket? He'll find out. Do a bit of shoplifting, with mother and father making quiet restitution? Not quiet enough, our Mr. Unrahh will find out. Or worse! Driving while intoxicated? Or a bit of reefer? Mr. Unrahh will uncover it. You see, sir, the Caesers are as close to perfection as humankind can get. Breeding, very careful breeding. Accordingly, we demand a proximity to our standards in those who would share the largess and honor of our name. Well, do you object?"

I smiled pleasantly, no small effort when you would like to have conked the other person on the head with a port bottle. "No, of course not. I'm grateful that my life has been thus far without official error."

He seemed unconvinced. "To be sure. Those are almost the exact words the late and somewhat lamented Timothy Hedgely used, sitting in that very chair. He, of course and wouldn't you know it, lied. He had hovered on the edges of alcoholism all his life. Had, as a teenager, spent some time in one of those chemical-dependency units. He said he had mastered it. He had not."

I stood to say good-bye but he was already on the phone. Kingsley was in the hall halfheartedly dusting at some treasure. I said, "How stands the nation, Kingsley?"

"There's to be a storm this evening, sir."

"Splendid!"

THIRTY-TWO

I tiptoed down the stairs to the basso rumble of thunder and the crashing static of electricity. It was 2:55 A.M. and the mansion was a dark and shadowy shroud. Lightning for a moment illuminated the faces of the lions and made them seem to come alive. That is all I need, I thought, two lions chasing me.

The rain began with a soft insistence, then increased until it was a blanket that covered everything in its path. Too late to turn back, I thought. Actually, it wasn't, but I had made up my mind, propelled by a sense of time—mine—ticking away. Even when I know or suspect my decision to be a bad one, I plow ahead. My father, in a burst of lingual activity, had predicted once that this very quality—he called it a habit—would wreck me. He said it as if I were an automobile.

My mother would smile and I never knew whether she agreed with him or me. She was the Switzerland of our little family unit and took no sides in the silent wars we fought. Nor was any victor ever declared. If his advice proved right and I made a fool or worse of myself, no recriminations were ever uttered, no apologies were offered or expected.

If, on the other hand, *I* was right, I never pointed it out. So in my world, there were no official winners or losers. We suffered or triumphed silently.

I was in the butler's pantry, where I opened the wall cabinet and began examining the labeled keys. My pocket flashlight traversed them key by key. What exactly would they call that security area that I wanted to see up close?

Then, suddenly, my heart physically left its moorings and leaped into my mouth—I could almost physically taste my heart—as far off, I heard the tinkle of a ghost piano. I was so afraid, I bit my knuckles and dropped the flashlight, grabbing for it frantically like a drowning man for a piece of rope. I got down on my hands and knees, feeling for it, when the melody took shape. "La Donna Mobilé" from that wondrous clock in the music room! I sat there on the floor, a half-crazed look on my face, and let my heart work its way back to its cavern in my chest. My hand found the flashlight and I stood and continued my search. It was on the bottom row, almost forlorn, off to itself: COMPOUND.

I took the set of three keys, shoved them in my jacket pocket, closed the cabinet, and headed for the front door.

L. L. Bean, courtesy of the Caesers, had clothed me for the occasion. I had on double-layer underwear, corduroy jeans, a chamois shirt, over which was a trail model vest and a Warden's parka and hood. On my feet were polar boots with felt liners and on my hands a pair of buckskin gloves.

I still was not prepared for the rain that belted me across the face as if a gorilla had slapped me. It felt like a dull knife gouging at my cheeks and my nose quickly became an icicle. All in all, L. L. Bean came through and I trudged down the small path, my flashlight leading the way like Rudolph's nose.

The trees whipped back and forth as if a madman was shaking them and I sank down into the snow with every step I took. The effort of going on was exhausting but it was too late to stop. I could not conceive of that.

I winced, cried aloud, and prayed at every bolt of lightning, certain that one would find me and fry me on the spot.

Finally, I stumbled against the fence, the two buildings inside looming like dark mountains. With trembling hands, I could barely find the keyhole. The key didn't fit and I experienced momentary panic. Suppose these were the wrong keys!

One down, two to go. The second didn't go in, either—too big. I uttered a silent prayer. I studied the remaining key, brought it to my lips for a good-luck kiss, and inserted it. It didn't . . . it didn't . . . it did. That key had been made for that lock and when the lock sprung open, I felt as if I were witnessing a miracle! I began to laugh like a lunatic.

I pushed at the gate, against the wind, and it slowly

opened. I felt my way along a narrow walkway whose outline could barely be discerned in the snow and went to the smaller of the two buildings.

Another lock, this one set in a heavy metallic door. Key number two went right in and I thought, I'm on a roll. The smallest victory was mighty in that raging storm and in the storm inside me.

I let my flashlight play about the room, which appeared almost empty. There was a metallic object that looked like a workbench with three holes in its front, two small, one large. I had no idea what I was looking at. It seemed totally functional and perhaps handmade.

My foot kicked at something and I almost died as the sound boomed around that peculiar room. It was a heavy bucket. Next to it, almost casually leaning against the wall, was a mallet, the handle wooden, the head iron.

The room was windowless, the walls completely tiled in white. The atmosphere was antiseptic. Along the room's perimeter ran a narrow trough that emptied into a drain set into the floor. There was a faucet and beneath it a fireman's hose coiled like a huge snake. And that was it.

I went back to the workbench for a closer examination. I got down on my haunches for a better look. It was made of iron and the section containing the three holes opened into two parts. When the parts were together, it could be locked. I looked through the holes, saw nothing. Just three holes punched in heavy iron. I saw, too, that the object was bolted to the floor.

I lifted the top part, extended an arm through one of the smaller holes, and then the other. I got down on my knees and stuck my head through the large hole. I turned and looked upward. If the top part was down and locked in place there would be no way I could . . . oh God. Oh my God. Please God.

I sat there in the numbing cold but didn't feel the cold. I was encapsulated in my own fear. I wondered why I wasn't screaming and knew that inside, in the most basic essence of me, I was shouting my soul out.

I made baby sounds. What was I trying to say? "Wah wah wah!" My lips contorted as they tried to give form to sound and mucus ran from my nose. I bit my tongue, tasted my blood, and screamed, "Noooooooooooooo!"

Then I lay down—fetal position, hand jammed into my mouth, while my upper leg beat involuntarily against my bottom one.

I clenched my eyes shut and wiped the blood from my face; the front of my jacket was stained with it.

Breath began to seep back into my lungs and for a moment I lay there, fishlike, gasping on a pier.

I pushed myself into a sitting position. The insides of my cheeks were raw from my teeth; my eyes rested quietly on that object of supreme horror.

Stocks: Salem variety. A place to lock witches, adulterers, in total constraint, arms extended forth in supplication, head thrust through a hole for hell.

I saw Timothy, poor Timothy, in those stocks, the Pillsbury Doughboy blubbering for his life, and I saw that mallet crashing into his forehead, and I saw the bucket catching his vomit, his blood, and his life fluids as he died hideously in that surgically antiseptic killing room. Then I saw someone turning on the hose and washing the gore into those troughs and down the drain.

Adieu, poor Timothy.

Adieu as far as life was concerned, yet not good-bye. In death, they were not half through with him. They had only begun.

Monsters, I said aloud without passion. There, I called them what they were. Someplace along the paths of that history they so loved to extol, they had crossed the line and become fiends. At someplace in early time, they had left the fraternity of mankind and reverted to antiquity when man ate man.

I felt calm. Now I knew and the veils dropping away

made the mystery just an ugly truth. A light had been shined into a dark place.

They were insane and addicted. I did not believe that they could do without the consumption of human flesh.

I stumbled from the killing room, locking the door behind me, and went to the larger building only a foot or two away. A motor hummed right under its eaves.

The door was freezing to my touch and I had to put a shoulder to it to push it open. It was as I expected: a big walk-in cooler with hooks hanging from pipes extending horizontally from the ceiling. I didn't want to look up but I had come too far to turn back, to close my eyes, to deny terrifying reality.

I shot my light about the room and there it was, almost solemn, hanging from a hook. It hung there, the remains of a carcass, like a side of beef that had neatly been hacked from. It looked like some kind of cocoon.

I approached it warily, like a cautious fighter might approach an opponent with a good left hook. I played the light over its surface and kept telling myself, It's just a carcass. There, at the base of the hook that held it, something hung like an obscene holy medal.

I stepped closer to where I could smell the odor of frozen flesh. It smelled like any other meat. I put my flashlight closer to the hanging object. It was a Phi Beta Kappa key, left in some kind of grotesque humor, as if it had been graded beyond U.S. Government Finest. But brightest, too.

So they had done more than slam Timothy into eternity; they had insulted his death with their haughty superiority.

Rage swept down on me; by now I had a bursting headache and my throat felt like it was closing up. I punched one gloved fist into another in frustration. Now my anger was as great as my fear and greater than either was my need to stop them, to end it, to get revenge for everyone down the years who had died so hideously so that the Caesers could live so grandly.

In a hoarse voice, I promised aloud: "I will do it."

THIRTY-THREE

Alas, life is different than the most fervent pledge. Things happen, and when I awoke about noon my throat was raw, as if it had been scraped with sandpaper, and I burned with high fever.

The Caesers hovered over me like a loving family with soups, homemade remedies, and earnest concern. Eleanor never left my bedside, sitting, patting my hand, wiping my feverish brow, and applying cold compresses in an attempt to lower my temperature.

Justin sat in a corner, face all grave concern, while Mrs. Caeser issued quiet instructions to Kingsley and the staff to ensure my comfort.

Blissfully, I slept my feverish sleep and when my temperature reached 104 degrees, the doctor was brought in from the village and began shooting antibiotics into me.

I groaned a lot and once they even had to hold me down as I thrashed about in a terrible case of cramps in every part of my body. I did not know whether it was day or night; I do know that the doctor remained by my bed, as well as a registered nurse to monitor my condition.

I believe I heard the word *pneumonia* and recall a discussion as to whether I should be flown to Bangor. The Caeser plane stood ready.

Then came Mrs. Caeser's excited voice, quite clear—I was wide awake without even knowing it: "Look! The fever's down to one hundred!" I opened my eyes, to see her and Eleanor hugging delightedly. Justin buried his head in his hands and began to weep with happiness.

My own parents could not have shown more love and concern. I wished with all my heart that I did not know what I knew.

When I awoke, some fourteen hours had passed and it was dark outside my window. I became aware that someone stood at the foot of my bed, arms folded, the soft sound of measured breathing. Mr. Caeser, whom, I suddenly recalled, I had not seen during my illness! His quiet manner made me wish that I was still unconscious.

"Good evening, sir," I said lamely. My voice was weak and it had nothing to do with my illness. I was terrified.

He suddenly turned on the lights, all the lights, and my room was thrown into a brilliance that caused my eyes to ache.

He spoke in an unaccustomed softness of voice. "I have something to ask you, Mr. Anderson, and I would strongly recommend that you answer me honestly, directly, without equivocation. I am obligated to warn you that any lie on your part will result in immediate and terrible consequences, consequences that you cannot even imagine. Do we understand each other?"

"Yessir," I whispered, still blinking in the light.

"Where were you in that storm?"

"Where was I?"

"Do not play with me, sir. And again, I warn you, do not lie. We know you left this house, went out into it. Kingsley found your drenched clothes in the closet, where you'd thrown them. You did not catch pneumonia in the music room."

"Pneumonia," I said, as if I'd discovered the disease. I was fighting for time, for an appropriate lifesaving lie.

"Where were you?" he hissed, coming closer to me, his angry face terrifying, a blood vessel pulsating in his forehead.

"I've been feverish, I've been . . ."

"God damn you," he roared, grabbing my pajamas and shaking me to and fro. "Tell me!"

"Outside, I was outside," I screamed.

"I know that," he shouted, hauled a great arm back and slapped me across the face, knocking my head back as if I'd been hit by a jackhammer. My jaw felt broken.

"I did go outside. I had to get out of this house. I needed to think." I began to blubber, hating myself for doing so, but just about out of control. I thought he might choke me to death. His hands opened and closed uncontrollably by his side.

"Think? Think about what? What did you need to think about in a storm?" He was about to strike me again. In my weakened condition, I did not know how much physical abuse I could endure.

"About lying!" I shouted. "About lying to you!"

"Yes. I do believe you are a liar. And worse. What had you lied about? And it better be good."

Here goes, I thought. "When you asked me in the library if there was anything in my past, I lied and I was too frightened to tell you."

He sat on the bed. It almost tilted over. He stared through me. Because their entire existence was a lie, surely they could understand someone else lying. "Go on," he said calmly.

"In high school, it happened in high school. I was arrested."

"Ah ha!" he barked. He sounded like a sea lion.

"I'm not proud of it. In fact, I'm quite ashamed," I said, pouring it on.

"I'm certain you should be." They were so damned certain. And brutal. And deadly.

"Marijuana."

"Selling it, no doubt. A business enterprise, eh?"

"No sir. Smoking it. In a car outside a high-school hangout. The police drove up and there I was."

"And?"

And what? I had no earthly idea. I didn't even smoke regular cigarettes. I wondered whether he could see my feet crossing and uncrossing beneath the covers. "The charges were never pressed. My family knew someone, a councilman, and it was my first offense. The judge talked to me in his chambers, scared me, warned me. I'm sure it's on file someplace and I figured your detective would uncover it."

"Of that you may be very sure."

"I just could not bring myself to tell you. I knew that it would wreck Eleanor and me." I wiped at my eyes. I was crying, but for my jaw, which ached terribly.

He was studying me intently. He reached for my hand and I thought, Oh Jesus, here it comes, but he only squeezed it paternally. "You're a mere boy. About what happened a moment ago—I do have a violent temper. I thought you might be a dirty little sneak, rooting about, trying to find out something about the Caesers. I will not have that. You do understand? Of course you do. Now get some sleep. You're quite pale."

The good samaritan tiptoed to the door and stopped. I closed my eyes and faked a snore. I heard him softly say, "Whatever shall we do with you?"

I thought, I, on the other hand, know exactly what I'm going to do to you. And I slept.

And dreamed of a Phi Beta Kappa key swinging in a dark breeze.

THIRTY-FOUR

"You look awful," she said. I, in pajamas and a robe, sat in her studio as she continued the sketch. "You're yellow like an Oriental and you look like you've lost half your weight. But you're still cute. Barely."

"You, on the other hand, are as adorable as ever and are still a bitch. Barely," I said. She liked it and stuck out her tongue.

Justin entered without knocking, looked at me, and began: "You look . . ."

"I know," I said, "Eleanor just told me. It's my recuperation therapy. That and a lot of soup should have me perfect in no time."

"He called me a bitch," Eleanor said.

"Well, he's certainly right about that," Justin said, ducking the charcoal she threw at him.

"Am I? Am I really?" she asked.

"You are. You really are," we both answered, as if we'd rehearsed it. We sang it.

"Thus is music made," Justin said.

"And genius heard," I said.

"Bullshit!" she said.

"What language," Justin said with mock shock.

"What a pair," I said.

"A threesome," Justin said, and it sounded more like a question than a statement. She looked at us as though awaiting an answer. I believe she was amenable, as amenable as he. Old-fashioned me (blast my father) wasn't having any, thanks.

"Believe I'll stick with a twosome," I said, smiling.

"He's dull, Justin, just dull," Eleanor said, not smiling.

"Give him time. He's wet behind the ears, stranger in a strange land, and all that. A little time."

"But does he have time?" she asked, and there they were at it again, discussing me as if I wasn't present.

We considered that matter silently. All of us smiling. Me the most.

A visitor at midnight. "Hello, Annabel Lee."

"You've been sick," she said, as if I didn't know it. "I've come twice but you were sound asleep. I thought about disturbing you. Would you have liked to be disturbed?"

"I'm not sure I'd have been up to it," I said.

"I'd have gotten you up . . . to it," she replied.

I changed the subject. "The Caesers have been wonderful."

"More than you deserved. We are a very caring people," she said. "Do you feel better?"

"Yes. Most of my strength's come back."

"I'm glad. I like you. You are, I believe, despite your paranoia, a kind man."

"Is that why you didn't do it?" I asked.

"Do? Do what? Are you still feverish?"

"Is that why you didn't tell your father about my . . . suspicions?"

"I didn't want to hurt you."

"What you mean is, you didn't want me to be hurt," I said.

"How silly! Who would want to hurt a silly boy with an overactive imagination, a writer, a dreamer, a seer of dark plots in everything. Your Rorschach must be a doozy."

"I don't believe you. I don't believe you wanted to see anything happen to me because you couldn't have pleaded innocent. You're a recluse; you didn't know. But you would have known because your words would have sent them after me. Hard to rationalize that."

"Why do you always attack me?" she asked. "It's not what I want from you!"

"Sorry, but I've got some needs, too. Physical release, sure. I'm fairly normal. You're an artist at it, you know you are. And yeah, I love it. Who wouldn't? But these other needs keep getting in the way," I said.

"Like what?"

"I'm going to sound like a DC comic. I want to see justice done. And that means the truth coming out, the dead avenged, and the guilty punished."

"The guilty being my family."

"Yes."

"You are one of the Hardy Boys!"

"Ah, what's the use. I'm getting a headache and my jaw is killing me."

"Close your eyes."

"I'm afraid to in this house."

"Do what I say," she said. I felt her breath on me, her hands foraging.

"Oh dear God. Oh God."

Polly looked worse, as if she had fallen into a vat of rye. Her now eggshell smock had picked up new smudges on the pockets and the elbows. There was less effort to cover the whiskey tracks on her face. Her hair was in disarray, wisps of it coming down over her eyes, and her hands held on to each other to control the shaking. I hated her weakness and I cursed myself for needing her.

She peered across the counter at me, as though I was standing on the other side of a river. She really didn't know who I was and my heart sank as I thought, What a start.

"Me," I said. "The one from the island." Something clicked.

"Wasn't sure I'd ever see you again." She laughed, only it sounded like a cough.

"I wonder if we can talk."

"See me later. Say next year. This is business hours," she said.

"Later, I'm not sure that I'll be around, and if I am, you probably won't be in any condition to listen."

"That's true. What is it you wanted to talk about?"

I figured I had one shot. "Your brother."

"L.C. is gone. What's there to say? What's it to you?"

"Don't you want to know what happened to him? Something did. As to what's it to me, I think I'm next on the 'something's going to happen' list."

"Hey, now you sound drunk!"

"That makes us equals," I said.

She let go of her left hand long enough to scratch her head. Her eyes were watery and she had the sniffles. She wiped a sleeve across her face. "Wait here," she said, and tottered to the front door, where she hung the CLOSED sign. "Come on," she said, and I followed her through an opening in the counter to a small storeroom. A few unopened cartons lay about in disarray.

Some coffee was brewing in one of those electric coffee makers. Next to it was a card table, a couple of chairs, a bottle of rye and glasses. "Coffee?" I nodded and she poured even as she reached for the bottle.

"Please wait. I want you to listen."

"Why, you . . ."

"I think my life may depend on it."

"Just one to start the old engine," she said, her back to me. She filled a glass and drank it down, waited for it to hit, sank into a chair, and again reached for the bottle.

"You said just one," I reminded her.

"So I did," she said, and motioned me to a chair. We sat opposite each other like players in a poker game. "You look awful," she said.

"I've been sick."

She nodded. "Pneumonia. I filled your prescriptions."

"Jesus," I said. She liked it and laughed, ending in a

horrendous cough. "Talk to me," she said, "but hurry, because I can't promise nothing. Make that anything."

"Let me begin by asking you some questions. Okay?"

She nodded, her eyes flitting to the bottle that stood there like a challenge. My problem was that I didn't know how to begin. I was in foreign territory, crossing a border never crossed. My glibness had abandoned me. "What's law enforcement like around here?"

She flicked something off a fingernail that had been bitten to a nub. She smiled. "I had the prettiest hands. Law enforcement, huh?"

"Yes."

"Well, Grace has a police chief and he has a couple of men, one part-time."

"Relationship with the Caesers?"

"Owned down to their handcuffs. The village can't afford to pay them but a few bucks. The Caesers supplement their pay, so they make decent wages. Then at Wilmut, that's the county seat, there's a sheriff. Third generation. Nephew of that ghoul Kingsley. Then there's the state police troop, about fifteen miles from here. The governor runs them. His law firm works for the Caesers. He comes to the island once a year to pay homage. The Caesers always use the occasion to make some big contribution to the state university, like a new music building, big-time stuff. And that's law enforcement, Caeser style."

"But could they turn their eyes from murder?" I asked.

"You are a very innocent young man." I wasn't insulted. It was the truth.

"So really, there is no law enforcement?"

"Not where that family is concerned. Oh, they go through the motions. Christ, they spent a ton looking for L.C. No one could possibly criticize their efforts. That's all it was, an effort, and letters of condolences. In other words, and do pardon my French, bullshit."

"So we're on our own," I said.

"Uh-uh, you're on your own. Me, I'm just the local drunk making small talk."

"But your brother . . ."

"One corpse to a family, thanks."

The icy fingers of desperation were beginning to nudge me and despair lay right across the line. Alone, I was totally helpless. She reached out and patted my hand. "Tell me about it."

I stood. "What's the use. You'll hit the rye."

"I'll do that anyway," she said.

I leaned forward, my hands braced against the card table. "I can barely say it myself much less to someone else, someone else who is only partially present."

"Sit down," she commanded. "You are going to talk and I am going to listen. But we're going to do it my way." She poured us each a drink. "Now have one. Have two." We drank silently. She watched me.

"The Caesers aren't like us."

"That, young man, is an understatement," she said, and cackled.

"Not just the money. They're not like anyone else, rich or poor. I don't know how they got the way they are." I shook my head, stammered: "I don't know how, I just . . ."

"Watch very closely," she said, and downed her drink, pointing to my glass. I drank.

"They're a family of cannibals."

She never batted an eye, nor was she trembling. "Go on."

"They had this supplier, or maybe they have a new one, God knows I hope so. He keeps them in . . . meat. Freshly murdered no doubt. They're very particular. But when there's a window of opportunity . . ."

"You are a Yuppie," she said.

"When there's a handy person, they do their own killing. They did it to L.C. I've seen what's left of . . ."

181

She stood up, her glass waving to and fro like a baton beating out a waltz. "I do not believe you."

"For God's sake, why would I invent something like that? What would I gain except a padded cell?"

"Unless you're a psycho," she said pleasantly.

"Do I look like a psycho?"

"I wouldn't know. Haven't known that many. Now drunks, I've known a lot of them. But look, you come in here, looking like a scarecrow, and tell me that not only was L.C. murdered by the Caesers but he was murdered so they could eat him! Now really. What in the hell do you expect me to believe? Besides, how do you know?"

"I saw L.C.'s remains."

She jumped, knocking a glass to the floor. "You what? What'd you say?"

"Back at school. In Justin's apartment, in . . ." I couldn't say it aloud because it sounded so bizarre anyplace but in my head. Then I thought, But it's true!

"You lost me. What was L.C., what was L.C.'s body doing in Justin's apartment?"

"Oh, there was no body."

"What are you doing?" she screamed, a hand around my collar.

"I'm trying to tell you and not doing much of a job."

She let me go. Her face was grim, her smock heaved with barely contained emotion. "Just say it."

"Justin has a deep-freeze. In it were some cuts of meat, wrapped and carefully labeled. Labeled L.C. I asked him what L.C. stood for. A certain herd in Argentina, he said."

She wasn't drinking now and someone was pulling on the front door. She made a motion that it didn't matter. I don't think anything mattered at that moment—not even rye. She shook her head. Her eyes bore into mine. "Anything else?"

"Yes. Timothy, Eleanor's fiancé."

"As in Timothy who walked into the ocean?"

"That one. What's left of him is in a walk-in cooler behind a fence on the island. He now looks like the remains of a side of beef, hanging there on a hook from the ceiling." I felt bile coming up in my throat. She poured me a drink and I sipped it.

"How do you know it's him?"

"Someone made a little joke of it. They left his Phi Beta Kappa key with the body."

"I don't know what to say," she said, turning her glass as if it were a prism giving off different colored light.

"I'm afraid that's not all," I said. Now I couldn't stop.

"I've heard enough."

This, I whispered, as if we were in the midst of a large throng. "Next to the walk-in cooler is a smaller room. It contains a stock and a sledgehammer."

"A what? What did you say?" She looked a hundred years old. We must have resembled freezing street people trying to get warm around a burning barrel.

"A stock, like they stuck the witches in back in Salem. That's where they did them in. I'm sure. Hit them in the forehead, butchered them like your friendly neighborhood meat market."

"Proof. Have you got any proof? Not, mind you, that I'd know what you could do with it. I mean, say you called the FBI. By the time they believe you aren't some loony . . ."

"I know," I said miserably.

She sat back, tilting the chair. "So there's nothing you can do. Nothing."

"Do you believe what I've told you?"

Her response was immediate. "Yes."

"Will you help me?"

"Hey, wait a minute!" she said. She looked afraid.

"But L.C.—"

"L.C.'s dead. I'm not."

"Oh, yes you are," I said.

"You fucking punk."

"I'm sorry."

"When did you get elected coroner, going around saying who's dead? Huh? Answer me!"

"You're right."

"Damn right I'm right." She drank to it.

"I'm truly sorry," I said. I felt miserable. Why would I hurt this pathetic creature? I felt small and cruel. I could only imagine how she felt.

"Suppose I am," she said. "Who is it bothering? No one. That's one good thing about being alone. There's no one to hurt."

"I'd better go."

"What are you going to do?"

"If you're in," I said suddenly, feeling a glimmer of hope, "I'll tell you. If not . . ."

"And what would being in take, huh? What are the stakes in this game?"

Nixon said it best when Eisenhower was vacillating about whether or not to keep him on the ticket. Fish or cut bait. It was that time.

"I want to rid the earth of them," I said.

"Jesus!" she exclaimed. "Do you have any idea how hokey that sounds? Rid the earth of them, oh my God."

"Believe me. I'm serious."

"Yeah. Okay. I can see that. How do I fit in? And before you tell me, I'm not promising anything. Better think that one over. In other words, if you tell me, you do it at your own risk."

I laughed. This was something brand-new. At my own risk. When in my life had I made a step with those consequences? What we do finally really does add up; there is a total.

"I need poison," I said. "Enough to kill four people."

Air escaped from her mouth like from a punctured tire. "It figures," she said.

I waited for more. We both waited. "Can you get me some?" I asked.

"I'm a licensed pharmacist."

"Will you?"

"No. I'm sorry. I can't do that."

"Why?"

"I just can't. You know how there are things we just can't do? Well, I can't knowingly take life. Any life. I don't hunt or fish. I step over roaches. I've always been that way. I have this reverence for all things except me. I lost that. Know who started a dog pound here? A damn good one. Me. Know who put up the money for it? You got it, your neighborhood monsters, the Caesers."

"I understand."

"So what'll you do?" The bottle was dead.

I grinned weakly. "Back to the old drawing board."

"You'll get yourself killed."

As far as I was concerned, the conversation was over. "I want to buy a couple of small gifts for Eleanor and her mother."

We moved back into the store: a proprietor and her customer. "This candy is very popular."

"Let me have a big box."

"Will I see you again? Will you be back?"

I paid her and didn't bother to answer.

THIRTY-FIVE

Mr. Caeser called for our attention by tapping on his wineglass with a fork. There was a pronounced smile between his mustache and his beard, and those wolfish white teeth glinted like diamonds lying in snow.

"I have an announcement, an auspicious one even in the annals of the Caesers, whose history can be documented back to the fourteenth century, the bloody fourteenth century of our sainted martyrs."

"Hear, hear," Justin said, and Eleanor clapped while Mrs. Caeser tapped on the table as if she were in the House of Commons.

Eleanor wore a shapely black silk crepe pants suit with a low-necked white chiffon blouse and cropped pants.

"Mr. . . ."—he had forgotten my name—"Anderson, Mr. Marion Anderson has asked for Eleanor's hand in marriage. I heard him out and then began that process by which we verify the worthiness of those who would become us. The process has unturned no flaw, no smear upon his youthful life that might in any way deem him unworthy of that which we may bestow. In accord, and before telling you my decision, I ask you, Eleanor, How do you feel about this man who would be your husband?"

We looked at her. "I wouldn't marry him if he were the last man on earth."

There was, to say the least, shocked silence. Then a smile began to play about her lips, and the smile became a giggle and then a laugh as all our laughter joined hers, as she took my hand, much like a referee lifting the hand of a triumphant prizefighter. She said, "Yes, I'll marry him."

Mr. Caeser wasn't finished. "And you, sir? How speak you?"

"I love her." I turned to her. "I love you, Eleanor."

"Is that all?" Justin asked. "Is that all a poet can come up with? No sonnet?"

Mrs. Caeser nodded. "Do go on."

"Be articulate," Mr. Caeser commanded.

"Eleanor, God knows I have little to offer but my love. But my love is great," I said. Now they were playing my game.

"How great?" Justin asked.

"Not as great as the Caeser name, I know nothing is that great . . ."

"Hear! Hear!" echoed about the room. They really agreed with that!

"But beneath the greatest star, there are lesser stars. I am a lesser star. My love, my feelings radiate nonetheless with all the power that star can give." I hung my head as if I was overcome with emotion. Shame had no limits; survival even fewer.

Mr. Caeser wiped away a tear with his napkin and I basked in the family's adoration. "Justin, what say you?"

"He will be the brother I never had," he said, and I thought, Here we go again.

"Dearest?" Mr. Caeser turned to his wife.

"His poetry will adorn this house," she said.

Mr. Caeser beamed. "Then it's done. He will be with us, brightening our lives." He stopped, then added almost as an afterthought, "So long as he may live."

"I feel just fine," I said, and all of us laughed.

"You've aged," Annabel Lee said. It was sometime after midnight and we sipped tea in her apartment while I decided how to tell her. I didn't know whether it would matter, whether she would care, whether I was hurting her. I didn't want to do that. I believe she had suffered enough for several lifetimes.

"It's the pneumonia. The fever. That'll age you."

"Yes, of course. That. But there are permanent wrinkles that weren't there when I first met you. Your eyes, beneath them and at the corners. Your eyes seemed to be crinkled all of the time. There's never any wonder or astonishment in them. They open only partially, like you've been squinting up into the sun. And your mouth, so set, like in concrete, even when you smile or laugh, your lips remain rigid, defensive. Your face seldom matches your words."

I was astonished at her perception. "I have changed."

"So quickly. Doesn't it usually take time?"

"I believe shock has a tendency to rush the process," I said.

"I'll get us some more tea," she said, and took the pot into the kitchen. I stood and walked to the heavily draped window and moved the drapes aside to get a look at the night. That would have been quite impossible, however. The drapes covered a solid wall. I heard her behind me.

"I require no window," she said. "I see enough."

She poured the tea and we drank it quietly. "Oh, I brought you something," I said, handing her a package. "It's very difficult to give the Caesers a gift. You have everything."

"Quite the contrary! We are the easiest people to give a gift to. We are always on the other end, the giver, and when someone thinks kindly of us, we all but swoon with delight. Would you like a chocolate cherry or a sugared almond?"

"Annabel Lee, I have something to tell you."

She examined the almond, pink in the wan light, and brought it to her mouth almost gravely, as if taking communion. "Good," she said, chewing. "Thank you for thinking of me."

"We're friends."

"I do my best within my limitations," she said, smiling in the direction of my groin.

"Me, too."

"What was it?" she asked, looking for another almond.

"Yes. I hope you'll understand. I have a feeling I'm letting you down, even betraying you, but it's not like it looks. Oh hell, I don't know how to say what I mean."

"Maybe you need a little relaxant."

"Eleanor and I are engaged."

She stopped chewing. There was a bit of pink sugar on her white lips. "Engaged in what?"

"Engaged to be married."

She swallowed, licked the crumb away. "I'm glad."

"You are?"

"Of course. That means you'll remain here with us. I like that. I do believe I need you."

"I'll be your sister's husband."

"And my sister will be your wife," she said, and smiled sweetly.

"And it doesn't matter?"

"Of course it matters! Makes it all the more . . . sexy. Wouldn't you say?"

"Excuse me. I'm not quite used to the law according to the Caesers."

"Oh but you will be. At first you'll be shocked, maybe even dismayed. You are very provincial. You'll have conscience pangs and an overwhelming desire to confess. You should a time or two, confess. And when you see that nobody gives a damn, except to envy you, you'll feel silly. And you'll not confess again. And finally, you'll understand the truth. Our truth. Not a general one, for goodness sakes! I'm not suggesting even for a minute that the world accept the Caesers' code. It wouldn't work, would it? In time, you'll love our way. You'll be a god. And you'll like that. Think of it, only one Commandment. We've thrown the other nine out. They're hardly viable."

"And that is?" I asked.

"Thou shall not betray the Caesers."

"No danger of that. The consequences scare me silly."

"Sit back."

"What?"

"Extend your legs. No goose, open them. I want to celebrate your entrance into our family. That's better. Do you like what I do?"

"I like what you do," I said.

THIRTY-SIX

I was on the second tier in the library when I suddenly realized that I was no longer alone. I pressed back into the stacks, peering down at Mr. Caeser, who had entered silently and was seated behind the desk, fingers nervously drumming on its surface. There was a fresh flower in his lapel and he looked as if he'd just come from the barber's, which was a joke. The barber came to them.

I started to clear my throat to make him aware of my presence when the door opened and Mrs. Caeser entered, walked around the desk, and kissed her husband's forehead. He reached up and squeezed her hand. Neither spoke and there was a quietness about them, a gravity of demeanor, that made me press farther back and remain silent.

He poured them each a glass of sherry, which they drank without saying a word.

It occurred to me that I was indeed Alice and that I had stepped through the looking glass, a feat much easier than stepping out of it. I watched this silent tableau, hoping that they could not hear my breathing, which had become labored in that quiet room.

His fingers increased their methodical drumming on the desk, like a soft tattoo in a funeral procession. She leaned forward, as if by body language to afford him support or comfort. He smiled at her, a timid smile, then looked down at his fingers, which he willed to stop.

"Dearest, perhaps you'd better tell me," she said.

He drank down the sherry and settled back in the chair, studying her as if she were someone new.

He nodded gravely. "Yes, I've no choice. What I'm about to say to you I've never said before, nor did we ever hear these words from our dear parents, nor our grandparents, God bless their souls. I am in despair and am experiencing no little shame."

"No!" she cried, and started to get up to join him.

He motioned her to remain seated and said, "I have failed." Then he stood, went to her, and lifted her face until it was looking up into his. "My precious wife, my beloved sister, my partner for life, I have tried. Oh God, but I have tried."

It was the first time I had ever heard the bravado gone from his voice. He was in despair and I wished I had had the nerve to applaud.

"I have exhausted my contacts, all of them. They are in abject panic, like a plague of fear has fallen over them," he said.

"But money!"

He turned from her in disgust. Now the old Caeser had returned. "A king's ransom!" he roared. "I've offered the moon. Shall I be specific? A million dollars. I hinted that ten million was not beyond the realm of possibility. Interpol, goddamn them to eternal hell, Interpol has sent them all scurrying like cowardly rats!"

"If Kalil is caught . . ." she began. Now she sounded frightened.

He smiled a tiny cruel smile. "He would have to be resurrected from the dead. Not likely that. Mr. Kalil's car went off the road in Brazil. The brake lining was in disgraceful shape. *Requiescat in pace.*"

"I never liked the man. Oily. He looked oily," she said.

"Nevertheless, an artist," he said.

"But the attorney, Kalil's papers?"

"Purchased. Mr. Kalil was of little material good from

the hereafter," Mr. Caeser said, examining his highly polished nails.

He sat down; his voice was almost drowsy. "Kalil was the best. Fresh, always so fresh. And tender. I shall miss him. The bastard."

They drank a silent toast to the departed.

"So where exactly are we?" she asked.

"We are where no Caeser has found himself in our lifetimes. With our backs to the wall. We are in the wall."

"Anything left?"

He waved that aside. "Two or three days at best, and that will have to be stews." He grimaced.

"It really is serious," she said, touching her cross.

"So what shall we do? We have to do something!"

"Shhh, you're shouting," she said. "Panic will solve nothing." She leaned forward across the desk. "There is the boy."

The boy wet himself.

Mr. Caeser said, "I rather like him. Innocent. Don't you?"

She shrugged. "I do like him, but I love survival."

"Eleanor's fiancé," he said.

They considered that and burst out laughing. He held up a cautionary hand. "I do believe Justin holds him in some affection," he said.

She smiled broadly. "Oh no doubt about that. They're buddies. Good buddies."

"And Eleanor?" he said.

"I don't know about that one. Eleanor belongs to Justin. She always has. She always will. It's the way."

He nodded. "The Caesers' way."

She said, "Still, I believe we should discuss the matter with them."

"By all means," Mr. Caeser said. "But I can only eat so much stew."

"You'd like a big roast, wouldn't you? Swimming in

gravy, rich dark brown gravy. I can taste it, I tell you. I can feel the meat's texture on my tongue." She licked at her lips.

"Do stop! You're making me famished," he said. "You know I've questioned myself. Wondered how our parents would have handled it."

"Exactly as we're going to. Remember the traveling salesman?" she asked. "We were mere children. We helped with him. I remember. You swung the hammer. You could barely lift it. Father had to finish him off. We were so excited! You were a boy and I was a child."

"A strong boy," he said, pride in his voice. "He felt very little pain. They soil themselves and they expire." The look on his face was dreamy. He basked in memory.

"I'll tell the children you want to talk to them after dinner," she said.

"Tell them it's a matter of some urgency."

THIRTY-SEVEN

Like the countdown for a rocket launch, I could hear the numbers being reeled off by mission control; see the second hand sweeping by on a big government-issue clock. Time: It had become the single-most-important element in my life and for my life.

I had little doubt that no Caeser would lift a finger of intervention in the cause of keeping Marion Anderson alive. They were a bloodthirsty, meat-hungry tribe and I was scheduled for their menus—a walking roast.

I was at once frightened out of my wits, feeling total

isolation, and yet, shared their desire for blood, except I wanted theirs.

I did not consider fleeing. I could not do that. This one time in my life, however long that was destined to be, I would do what my mother called the right thing.

The right thing knew the consequences but put them aside. That's how knights must have set out after dragons.

We spend our lives picking up tricks—either consciously or subconsciously—in how to survive. There's always a voice whispering in our ears: Everything's going to be okay. Even as we die, I believe we hear that voice. However, the only voice I heard was my own and it was shouting "Help!"

Nor was there a cavalry over the hill. No bugle. No troops. Me and them. I felt exhausted, as if I had run a long and losing race. No one waited in the stadium for me to cross the line. There was no line to cross.

I tied my black tie, staring at myself in the bathroom mirror. Could I go out and face them? I looked frightened! They would probably attribute that to my recent illness. Even pneumonia has its uses.

Suddenly, I lurched forward, head spinning, and caught myself on the marble washbasin. Fear is so tangible. Doom is no abstract.

I went down the stairs, patting my lions. I could hear the family in the great hall and as quickly as I entered, Kingsley handed me a glass of champagne. At least I was going first class! They sat like pieces on a chessboard. They didn't look of these times but resembled a faded yellow photograph of royalty posing for an official picture.

Mr. Caeser looked like some mad monarch against the shadows cast by the flames from the fireplace.

Then I realized the lights were dim and I wondered whether they'd kill me right there and roast me. It was so theatrical, and, sadly, I knew the role assigned me. Was the play tonight? Had they hurried their schedule?

Mr. Caeser spoke. "This is a special evening. All the family is here and I love it that way."

I didn't understand what he was getting at until I saw Annabel Lee sitting among them like a statue, glacial, distant, unreal. The flames made gray shadows on the alabaster surface of her skin. She seemed composed, as if being among people was quite natural.

"Annabel, this is Mr. Marion Anderson. Eleanor's fiancé. And this, young man, is my daughter Annabel."

I took her cool hand and she smiled a perfunctory social smile and said stiffly, "So glad to meet you, Mr. Anderson."

"And I you," I said, bowing.

"Well, what do you think?" asked Eleanor.

"Heavens, Eleanor, you're making our Marion blush," said Justin.

Mrs. Caeser smiled her approval. "Don't be such an old prune, Justin, look at your friend. He loves being inspected!"

"Well?" Eleanor insisted.

"He's quite presentable," Annabel Lee said.

"That's all? Presentable?"

"Oh very well, Eleanor. He's quite presentable. In fact, he's rather good-looking in a boyish way."

I smiled.

Annabel Lee said, "There, you see. Most attractive."

"Thank you," I muttered.

"A toast to my precious daughters," Mrs. Caeser said. She sounded like any proud mother and I reminded myself that she was also their aunt.

We drank champagne to them.

"And now let us retire to dinner," Mr. Caeser said, and offered his arm to his wife. I escorted the sisters on my arms, with Justin bringing up the rear and singing some German drinking song that must have been lewd. The family laughed and I joined in.

God knows the chef had made every possible effort to make the stew look like something else. Its sauce—a red wine—was delicate to behold, and it had been garnished with things that I didn't even recognize. I stuck to my poached fish.

Eleanor led the critique. "The pits."

Nor was Justin overwhelmed. "Jesus . . . I mean Jesus!"

Mr. Caeser sought no out. He hung his head in guilt. Mrs. Caeser comforted him as best she could.

Annabel Lee was the peacemaker. "Now do you see why I remain in my apartment? Can't we enjoy some semblance of tranquility?"

"We'll discuss the matter later," Mrs. Caeser said, casting sidelong glances my way.

"That doesn't help now." Eleanor pouted.

"Later," Mr. Caeser said, and that ended the subject.

Conversation lightened when Justin informed them that we had finished this version of the show. They applauded and Justin stood and gave mock bows to each of them. I lowered my head in fake humility, at which I was becoming so adept.

They really liked it and Eleanor pinched my ear until it was red. "Don't you think he's adorable?" she asked her sister.

I sat between the two. I didn't understand the relationship between them. I understood it even less a moment later when I felt Eleanor's hand on my right thigh, followed by Annabel Lee's on my left. I did not believe it.

Both hands began foraging and when they met, engaged in fake combat with a lot of finger twisting right above my groin.

A kind of silent, fierce truce was entered into as they took turns fondling me, all the while listening with rapt attention to one of Mr. Caeser's interminable lectures, this one on the despotism of England's kings and queens, all of them to the present day. His dislike was such that you had the feeling that he had personally suffered at their hands, beginning with the fourteenth century, which was some kind of benchmark in Caeser family annals.

Mrs. Caeser smiled sensually at her daughters and I knew that she knew what was going on beneath the table. Justin sat grinning, giving nods and winks of approval.

Immediately following dessert, I, with hands in my pockets to cover my screaming needs, excused myself. I had not quite regained my health and they offered no objections. In fact, they seemed relieved at my departure.

I rushed to the library, climbed the stairs, and hid behind a shelf, removing one fat tome so that I could look down without being observed.

One by one, they straggled in, with the exception of Annabel Lee, and positioned themselves around the desk occupied by Mr. Caeser.

"Did anyone see where your young friend went?" asked Mr. Caeser. "He seemed to be in an awful hurry."

"Probably to his room to masturbate," Eleanor said. "We drove him crazy."

"We?" Mrs. Caeser asked.

"Our Annabel joined right in, thank you, without so much as a 'by your permission.' He is *my* fiancé," said Eleanor.

"Oh, I'm so pleased," Mrs. Caeser said, hugging her daughter. "Annabel gets so little out of life. Justin, you should try—"

"I do, Mother, I do. The girl is just plain oral," Justin said.

"Aren't we all," Mrs. Caeser said. "But do keep at it. The girl needs a man."

"And you are that," said Eleanor, kissing her brother on the mouth. I could see an exchange of tongues.

"Oh, stop," said Mrs. Caeser. "You're making me wet myself." She then slipped a hand down her daughter's bodice.

"Wait. It'll have to wait. More important matters at hand, the most important!" Mr. Caeser said.

He ran them like a ringmaster runs a circus. You could see their obscene sexual activity stop immediately. He even controlled their moods. He did give them a moment or two to gather themselves. They sat quietly.

"I've failed," he said. "Wait, no interruptions, no comfort. I do not shy from truth. There is simply only one available at this moment to supply our needs for sustenance. This cruel and infamous investigation by Interpol has stopped all creative activity, and do believe me, I've searched the world over, even considered, God help me, Kingsley. I cannot, will not, feed my family a diabetic. Nor a servant. Standards, that's what we're about. Standards. Mind you, I did consider Orientals, perhaps one of those energetic Japanese. I could not."

"He tried so, poor dear," Mrs. Caeser said.

"Which leaves us no place," Eleanor said.

Justin moaned. "It really is serious. One more stew and I'll vomit on the table. It's not only making me nervous, but my allergy has broken out. Look," he said, removing his jacket and rolling up his sleeves, displaying an arm mottled with ugly red and white splotches.

Mr. Caeser nodded grimly. "I'll be the same way by tomorrow."

"I'll look horrible," Eleanor shrieked. "My face will break out and my breasts. My *breasts*, for God's sake!"

"What ever shall we do?" asked Mrs. Caeser.

"What we must," Mr. Caeser said. "The Caesers must endure."

No one said anything. They just sat there, looking uneasy. Finally, after waiting for someone else to speak, Mr. Caeser said, "I do like the boy. He's excellent company and no trouble at all."

Justin said, "I've grown rather fond of him."

"We are all fond of little Marion," Mrs. Caeser said.

"Then not only are we faced with a problem but a problem compounded. Still we must reach a decision. One based on a single criterion," Mr. Caeser said.

"The survival of this family," Justin said.

"Well that's your decision, isn't it?" Eleanor asked.

Mr. Caeser sighed sadly. "Yes, that's it. I'm sorry, Justin."

"We all are. But there's simply no other way, is there?" Justin asked. Nobody answered him.

Mr. Caeser clapped his hands as if summoning a genie. "Well then, it's settled!"

"Let's get on with it," Justin said.

Mrs. Caeser kissed his cheek. "There's no need for you to participate."

"Certainly not," Mr. Caeser said.

"Well you're going to eat, aren't you?" Eleanor asked.

Justin drew back his arm as if he was going to strike her. "Bloody bitch!"

Mrs. Caeser stepped between them. Mr. Caeser appeared amused. "See what hunger does to us? Makes us animals. Can you imagine, the Caesers animals?"

Everyone settled down. Justin said, "Of course I'll participate. It's my duty."

Mrs. Caeser beamed. "He's a Caeser, that one."

"When?" asked Eleanor. "Let's do it now! I'm starving."

Mr. Caeser said, "No. Tomorrow after dinner. A fine meal, the finest wines."

"I'll just bet he's tender," Eleanor said, "the tenderest we've had in ages. Timothy was tough."

"Oh, my mouth is watering," Mrs. Caeser said.

"It is exciting," Mr. Caeser said, "in every way."

"You men," Mrs. Caeser said, dropping her hand in Justin's lap.

"Not here," Mr. Caeser said. "Let's retire to the bedroom. I do believe Eleanor needs a good spanking. She's been a very rude girl."

"Yes, that's what I need. Hurry!"

THIRTY-EIGHT

It was as if she had been standing there waiting for me. I had barely raised my knuckles when her door swung open and she stepped aside to let me enter. I felt lifeless, drained of all the juices that made me a human being. I sat slumped, staring at her, having no idea whether or not even to say anything.

I cleared my throat, not knowing whether it was even working. What was I doing here? What would she do? Was she capable of even the most basic human response?

"What is it?" she said.

I tried to speak but nothing came out. It was as if my vocal cords had frozen. I grimaced piteously. She poured me a beaker of brandy and I gulped it down, letting the fierce liquid burn my throat into speech.

"Help me," I said hoarsely. I had run out of words. I was down to childish basics.

"Tell me." Her face was cold.

"They're going to kill me." I began to cry like a baby. Her response was to pour more brandy, but I was afraid to swallow it because of the sobs wracking my body. She held the glass to my lips and I sipped it. My face was against her thigh and her other hand held my head in support.

"Who's going to kill you? You've got to get hold of yourself."

"The Caesers. The Caesers are going to kill me."

"That's insanity," she said, but it sounded as if she was doing a selling job on herself.

"No, it's true. Please believe me. Won't you believe me?" I was begging and sobbing and sipping my brandy all at once. My voice rasped as if I had been screaming, and perhaps I had, but inside. Can one scream silently? Oh yes, just as one can bleed internally.

"You'll have to go unless you stop that ridiculous wailing. I am not a handkerchief," Annabel Lee said.

"I'm sorry, I'm sorry," I said as a tremor shook me. "I was in the library, you know the library . . ."

"Yes! I know the library."

I smiled gratefully. She sat down.

"They were all there."

"They? My family."

I nodded eagerly, as if I was making great progress. "They need . . . they need sustenance . . . the Caesers' kind of sustenance."

"It's a very human need."

I shook my head. "Not human meat."

"That."

I was astonished. No denial. No telling me I was crazy. "How . . . how . . ." I tried to phrase my question.

"Hmmm. I don't know," she said.

"Please!" I begged.

"We do not tell it. Ever."

"What difference can it possibly make?" I asked.

She smiled warmly. "None, I suppose."

"None at all. I am a dead man."

"Poor Marion."

"Yes, poor me."

"I suppose it can't hurt to tell you. Perhaps you deserve to know."

I nodded.

"One stipulation. I want you to sit there and not open your mouth. Understand? No comments. No judgments."

I nodded.

"We'll have to go back, way back. Scotland and the

fourteenth century. James I was king. The country was in turmoil because people were disappearing. Merchants and travelers. Accusations were made and some innkeepers were hanged. But the disappearances went right on. Then, one night, a farmer and his wife were returning from market when they were attacked by a ragged, blood-smeared band. They cut the woman's throat and drank her blood, but the farmer managed to get away. The king was notified and he responded with soldiers and bloodhounds. A manhunt began. Too much for you? Nod your answer."

I shook my head no.

She smiled. "The band was tracked down to a cave by the seashore. In it, they found smoked and pickled human limbs and a treasure. A vast treasure. And you'd better have some more brandy." She poured.

"The cave's occupants were captured, bound, and brought before the king. Interrogation disclosed that the band were members of a single family led by one Sawney Bean. Does the name mean anything to you? No, of course not. It's in every library. Under legends, I believe. But the Bean family was no legend. You could verify that, couldn't you? Nod."

I did.

"Anyway, it seems that for years this family had lived by highway robbery and, of course, cannibalism. How they fell into that—shall we call it taste or predilection?—is lost to history. No trial was held. The group's guilt was obvious. The men were burnt at the stake in Edinburgh, their women forced to watch. The women then had their hands and feet cut off and they bled to death. So, the legend goes, that was the end of the Sawney Bean clan." She tossed down her brandy.

"Except it wasn't! A little boy and his sister escaped. How, is not known. But, thank God, thank all the gods, they did. That brother and sister are my ancestors. Now you know and you may speak."

"Cannibalism . . . incest . . ."

"Think of it as our lifestyle; that'll make it terribly modern and easier to digest. Or our civil rights, can't deny us those, can you? I'm quite certain it began with necessity. Even the wretched poor of Scotland had to eat, didn't they? Human flesh was available, indeed in great quantity. Over the years, the evolutionary process took over, like man slithering in from the sea and over time developing little flippers that today we call arms and legs.

"As for incest—naturally, that's what you call it—we chose to love those who shared our needs and whom we could trust. Our own kind. Nor has it produced any monsters. We are, except for my rare disease, which science calls Xeroderma pigmentosum, quite normal, normal by our standards. As you may or may not know, my parents are brother and sister. And the future?

"Justin and Eleanor will breed and a new generation will be born. We'll find a husband for Eleanor, drawn by her beauty and our wealth, and they will marry and he will be positive that he fathered their child. A Caeser. That will, of course, be out of the scientific question. His food will be laced with a tasteless chemical that will render him quite sterile and he'll never know it. I predict he will give out cigars, Cubans, like Castro used to smoke.

"Well, poor dear, you're in quite a state, aren't you? You wanted to know."

I struggled to my feet; my legs felt watery. "I thought you were different."

"You really are a bit of a fool. I'm a Caeser."

"Yes."

"Is that it?" Her arms were folded across her chest. Deep within her black eyes, I could see tiny pinpricks of light. Her breathing was heavy.

"It is for me."

She stepped closer. "Let me do you."

I needed to strike out. "You and your sister, Jesus, what a couple of whores!"

She threw back her head, her white hair tossing from side to side with her laughter. "Whores? Quite the contrary. Just a couple of normal American girls, or would you call us gals?"

Her laughter followed me down the hall. Time was running out and I had one more suspicion to confirm. I knew that I would never have another chance. I needed to know it all.

I entered Eleanor's studio and turned on the light. I took a long look at what she considered her masterpiece. To me, it looked like pink Silly Putty spread out on a canvas. I ran my hand over its layered surface, stood back, squinted my eyes, opened them, studied it, turning my head from right to left and then back again.

I knew what it was.

Flesh.

It consumed them. They were propelled by madness and hunger.

The two paintings, covered so carefully, stood innocently on their easels. I had this feeling . . . my hand shook as I uncovered the first.

A great roar of breath burst from me at still another shock in this house of murder.

Timothy in pastels. Timothy at the moment of maximum terror, aware that this moment, captured so perfectly, would be his last as a living creature.

His cheeks bulged as if he were blowing a trumpet and the tip of his tongue lay against the side of his mouth like an eyeless fish. His eyes were rolled back into their sockets, the pupils peeping down like quarter-moons. I could hear him screaming.

His sparse hair was plastered down on his forehead in wet bangs, like some kind of obscenely seductive hairstyle. His face was covered with tiny ringlets of sweat that seemed to be popping out through open flesh.

"Oh Timothy," I said aloud, and dropped the canvas.

Not that it mattered. As long as I lived, and I knew that would not be long, I would see his face.

Rest in peace, Timothy.

I removed the next covering. It was Lafcadio Charles Kole, whom I had never seen, face put back together by doctors who didn't have to live with it. It was a second-rate job. The face was split in half, a long puckered scar the line of demarcation between the parts that would never again fit.

The look was different from Timothy's.

There was no horror beyond the horror of the surgery. Instead, there was a look of unfathomable sadness and bewilderment. He didn't get it and that made it all the more sad.

Eleanor had perfectly captured that face of terrible innocence.

I was overwhelmed with unspeakable sorrow at what had befallen these two whose crime was falling into the hands of vile creatures from hell.

I left that grotesque gallery, muttering softly to myself a prayer that made no sense but told how much I mourned them.

THIRTY-NINE

On the surface, the day was like the days that had preceded it. The wind called and waves crashed and bits of snow fell almost apologetically to the frozen earth.

Kingsley expressed a "Tut tut" that I would pass on

breakfast. I smiled an appreciative smile that he cared and he stared back with perplexity.

I spent a good part of the morning staring out the front window. Except for the elements, nothing moved. It was as if we and our world had been captured in a photograph and had no life.

I listened, too, to the ocean as it crashed over and over like a recurring auto wreck. It would go on that way forever. It did not need me for an awed audience. It played its music for itself.

At two, I entered the music room, where Justin sat as usual behind the piano. There was a difference. He stood and extended a hand and clasped mine with solemn formality like the first time we had ever met. I had the feeling that he would have liked to embrace me but couldn't come up with an acceptable rationale.

After all, it was a day like any other, wasn't it?

"I have some good news," he said, but there was no joy in his voice.

"And that's how I'll always remember you, Justin," I said.

"Oh?"

"Bearer of good news. You always know something good is coming. You would have been the first settler to sense the cavalry coming from over the hill."

"There's no cavalry," he said. Oh how I would have liked to wipe the smile off his patrician face with a piece of jagged glass.

"The news, the news!" I said, playing out our farce.

"On Monday, we go to New York. To the Plaza."

I thought, How cruel. Is there no end to their cruelty? I wished them ill. Much, much ill.

"We'll stay as long as it takes. We'll have the right contacts; some investment bankers that do business with the family will see to that. Everyone we want to hear our show will hear it! Nor will we stand in line or kiss the backsides of Jews named Saul or Louie," he said.

Then I realized what he was doing.

He was giving me a kind of gift, a whiff of a delicious fresh-baked cake that I would never taste.

"It sounds unreal," I said. "Like a fantasy."

"I assure you it's quite real, I . . . we leave on Monday!" A minor slip. "I'm overwhelmed," I said. "The Caesers are a people of miracles."

His face was stern, as if he was lecturing himself. "We are a people who do what we must and have the where-withal to do exactly that."

We were smiling at that truth when there was a hesitant rapping at the door. Kingsley entered, holding a package wrapped in brown paper and string.

"What have we here, Kingsley?" Justin asked.

"It's a package, sir, from the village. It's for Mr. Anderson," Kingsley said.

"Oh! Were you expecting anything?" Justin asked me.

"That's what I've learned from the Caesers," I said. "To expect anything."

"Open it," Justin said to Kingsley.

I exploded. "Hey, I believe that's addressed to me!"

"Open it," Justin said, as though I had not spoken. Kingsley immediately complied with his master's voice.

"Well? What is it?" Justin asked.

Kingsley held it up. "A bottle of French perfume, sir."

Justin was all smiles. "You sly devil, you. Something for Eleanor. What a generous fellow you are."

"I do my best," I said, "and sometimes believe in God."

"Well, don't just stand there, Kingsley, give him his per-fume," Justin said, and Kingsley ceremoniously handed me the package as if he was bestowing some minor order on me for some minor accomplishment.

Kingsley left us. Justin put his arm about me. "You're angry, aren't you?"

"That was my package," I said. "My surprise. Surely there are some rights, even in this house."

"Rights? Hmmm, I don't know about those. Consider it one of our little peculiarities. Forgiven?"

"Of course," I said. Our eyes locked. I do not know whether he believed me.

"Then on with our work," he said.

"Yes! Our work."

FORTY

How resplendent they were! How regal. They stood as if frozen in time, chandelier lights bouncing off diamonds.

Eleanor was a dream—or a nightmare—in a tiered dress with satin ribbons and lace ruffles on organza. Several decorations adorned Mr. Caeser's lapel, no doubt from grateful governments that had enjoyed his legendary largess. He looked like a king, not like Santa Claus but like Henry VIII, monumental and full of leashed power, greeting me with a hug and thrusting a glass of champagne into my hand.

"This one still looks pulled down. Oh, we'll have to fatten him up," he boomed.

Mrs. Caeser kissed me lightly on the lips and Eleanor kissed me with such passion that Justin said, "Puleeze!" We laughed. We all laughed. The great hall resounded with familial warmth, of which I was the object. I was being showered with love. And farewells.

They stood about me, hanging on my every word, clapping my back, squeezing my hand, as if I were on show at Westminster.

"He's perfect," Mrs. Caeser said, barely hiding her tongue licking greedily at her lips.

"He'll do in a pinch," Justin said as his sister pinched my butt, and oh how we laughed!

"Drink up, drink up," Mr. Caeser commanded me, and I followed his command while they applauded as if I had performed wonders.

Mr. Caeser nodded gratefully. "Simply one of those special evenings. I can tell! Come Kingsley, Mr. Anderson's glass is empty. I do believe you're slowing down." Then he winked at Kingsley to let him know it was just a joke.

They were pouring champagne down me.

Justin asked, "Isn't it astonishing? We can all feel it. It's like . . . well, a beginning! It's delightful!"

I had no idea what was delightful but I gave him a happy wave.

"Can you feel it?" he asked me.

"Oh yes," I said. "I can definitely feel it." They applauded! I was quite obviously a prince among men.

Mr. Caeser said, "Describe it."

"Describe it?" I asked.

"You are the one with the words, aren't you?" asked Eleanor.

"Yes, I am that one!"

"Well?" Justin demanded.

"I feel . . ."

"Go on," Mrs. Caeser urged. They were peering at me. They really had an urge to know.

"I feel excited," I said.

"Yum yum," said Eleanor.

"And curious? Suddenly I want to know everything! Like . . . how the world will end. Am I mad?" I asked.

"I believe the word is drunk," Justin said.

I did feel drunk, but not bad drunk. I wanted to be more drunk; oblivion. "I want more," I said.

"Ah, but we all do," Mr. Caeser said. "Small men call it greed. We call it passion. Life's sweet passion."

"I am very passionate," I said, and they nodded gravely and exchanged looks.

"Sir," said Kingsley, "dinner is served."

"Not quite," said Mrs. Caeser, and as she went by, I heard her add, "Not quite."

Five abreast, like Robin Hood's merry band, we went from the great hall into the dining room. Friar Tuck was holding me up. What was Friar Tuck doing here and why was he holding me up? A friar would do such kindness, I thought. Then he was helping me into my chair, tucking a napkin about me, placing my wineglass in my hand, then standing back, hands on fat hips, and saying, "There," as if I had taken all my ba ba. They were smiling. I was much loved. I was a good baby.

I stared transfixed, my eyes glassy but fixed on the serpent on the Fabergé decanter, much like Eve must have looked at that first snake.

Dark amber wine was being poured into their greedy glasses.

"None for me," I said. "Thank you, but I'm feeling whoops!" And my head fell forward on my chest.

Justin said, "Here here!" And Eleanor said, "Whoops, whoops!"

"Well, I've never heard it called that before," Mrs. Caeser said, and I gaily joined in: "Whoops! Whoops!"

The room was a chorus of "Whoops!"

Justin proclaimed me "King of the Whoops," and they toasted his majesty, to which I stood up and bowed on crazy legs before falling back into my chair.

Mr. Caeser stood. "On this special evening, we honor our dear one, Marion, who unfortunately does not seem to be able to hear me, our dear one who will make it all possible, giving us the greatest gift that man can bestow upon man. By his noble sacrifice, he will enable a great family to do that for which they were bred: endure. Surely no man could give more than . . . his life."

They drank solemnly. My eyes were closed. I was about half-asleep.

"His departure gives us no pleasure. We are not savages; we do not desire the death of any man. But sometimes . . . sometimes, man is called forth to do great deeds for the common good. Dear Marion has been so summoned."

He was overcome by his words and had to wipe away a tear. Mrs. Caeser patted his arm and they grabbed each other's hands.

My mind stopped and I fell asleep. I don't know how long they sat there drinking and observing my narcoticized slumber. I was dimly conscious of being bodily lifted from my chair, and off, far, far off, a voice—I think a woman's voice—said, "Shouldn't we put on his coat. He'll catch his death of . . ." And there was much laughter.

In my leaden sleep, I smiled.

Then someone, a giant—it had to be a giant—slapped me across the face with a sting that burned me awake and I knew that I was outside in the freezing night and was moving though I could not move.

I was looking up at the stars, which seemed at hand. If I had had the strength, I could have reached up and plucked them like apples.

I was in a large wheelbarrow being pushed and pulled along through the snow and they were a jolly group of children, chattering and giggling even in their exertions, children playing in the snow.

Then I remember kneeling and it occurred to me that I was at prayer and I began to pray. "Our Father, which art . . ." Then I was awake.

"The night air brought him to," Mrs. Caeser said.

I was in the stocks and heard the sound of running water, and saw the water passing through the troughs like a merry brook on a summer day.

Mr. Caeser removed his jacket. Kingsley, ever the good servant, folded it across his arm.

"How can you do this?" I asked. "How can you do such a thing?"

"There'll be no pain, old boy," Justin said. Eleanor said, "Oh get on with it."

"Before we all freeze to death," Mrs. Caeser said, and hugged herself in her floor-length sable.

Mr. Caeser held out a hand like a surgeon and Kingsley gave him the mallet.

Mr. Caeser lifted it like a baseball player selecting the right bat, as I gave up and prepared myself for death.

"Good God," Mrs. Caeser said, "he's wetting himself!"

"No class. The kiddo's got no class," Eleanor said.

Mr. Caeser lifted the mallet high in the air and took a few practice swings, which all eyes followed. Then the mallet fell from his hands and he stared down at it stupidly, unable to do anything with his fingers, which had no feeling in them.

"What is it?" he asked, but there was no answer because now they were all feeling it, except Kingsley, who over and over said, "Sir? Sir? Sir?" And he made nervous little steps like a banshee.

They began to waltz: gliding in and out of each other as if on ice, touching, barely touching each other on the arm, on the face, trying to speak, not being able to. They were trapped in a kind of dreamy adagio.

Justin slumped to the floor first, sitting, his bottom half in the trough, his arms trying to enfold himself against the cold that was settling over him.

He tried to focus his eyes, to look at me. He unlocked his arms with great exertion and pointed at me, a frozen hand that dropped into his lap. His eyes went up as though he were trying to stare through his skull. Then they fluttered and closed.

He seemed at peace.

I thought of an Oscar Wilde couplet: "The dead are dancing with the dead. The dust is whirling with the dust."

Mr. and Mrs. Caeser approached each other like wrestlers trying to get a hold. Their fingertips touched and they almost made it to an embrace but slipped to the floor, gently, so gently, staring ahead, eyes now glassy, then closed shut, instantly, like a camera shutter. They died a foot from each other.

Eleanor stood straight up, her back braced as if at attention, a soldier-girl in an old forties film. Her arms were straight down at her side, her fists clenched. She tried to open them; I could see the effort. She looked down at them in astonishment, amazement on her gorgeous face. A tiny trickle of blood made its way from her ruby lips. Then she spun about, twirling in a pirouette, then slammed face-down to the tiled floor, shook, and lay still.

Now there was only Kingsley, his eyes stretched wide, spittle down his face. "What have you done?" he screeched like a eunuch, grabbing me by my exposed throat. "What have you done?"

"I've done my duty; I've sent them to eternity." I forced the words from my mouth.

"I'll finish it," he said softly, increasing the pressure from his very strong fingers.

"Better hurry," I said. "The police know everything. They'll be here any second."

"Liar! Murderer!" he screamed.

"Let me go!" I gasped. I was going fast, my chest heaving like bellows as he increased the pressure on my Adam's apple. I had a second or two at most. I was dying. With the strength remaining in me, I said, "There's no need for you to be involved."

I felt his fingers uncoil one by one. He stepped back as I breathed in precious air and coughed and spat my way back into life.

He sat on the floor, weeping. "It's over," he said.

"It really is," I said. "Get me out of this thing."

FORTY-ONE

I visit Polly sometimes. She's in a home and she's still drinking but doesn't look any different. I've asked her about the poison; we don't call it that. We call it eau de cologne. She won't tell me the recipe.

"You have proven yourself to be a dangerous man," she says.

I laugh. I will never be dangerous again.

Kingsley has made an excellent butler for the warden at the state penitentiary. I tried to get him the death penalty.

The ghost still haunts that house. She refused to testify at the coroner's hearing or at the trial and her disease kept her from having to do so. However, they took her deposition and, amazingly, she told the truth.

I've taken a civil service examination and am awaiting the results.

It will be dull—very, very dull.

Thank God.

AUTHOR'S NOTE

The story of the Sawney Bean family can be found in most libraries. Xeroderma pigmentosum (XP) is a very real disease. Dr. Kenneth Kraemer, a research scientist at the National Cancer Institute in Bethesda, Maryland, is the foremost expert on it.